THE NONESSENTIALS

Z. MARTIN BROWN

Pathogen Press

Copyright © 2023 by Z. Martin Brown

All rights reserved

No part of this publication may be reproduced, distributed, or transmitted in any form or by any means, including photocopying, recording, or other electronic or mechanical methods, without the prior written permission of the author or publisher (other than for review purposes) except as permitted by US copyright law. For permission requests, contact Pathogen Press at pathogenpress@gmail.com.

The story, all names, characters, and incidents portrayed in this production are fictitious. No identification with actual persons (living or deceased), places, buildings, and products is intended or should be inferred.

Cover art and design by Jane Kirt

First Edition

ISBN: 979-8-9893760-0-1 paperback

ISBN: 979-8-9893760-1-8 ebook

Pathogen Press

www.pathogenpress.com

To Minae, for your unwavering belief in me

What you are now, we once were; what we are now, you shall be.

— Unknown, Capuchin Crypt

1. On a clear day, not today

My morning's been one shitty chain reaction after another, and I can't for the life of me get back on track. It started with me sleeping through my alarm, resulting in a frantic, no-shower, no-brushing, no-breakfast, no-caffeine run out the door late for work, and now I'm miles from my clinic, surrounded by clotted traffic. I need a zap of light to calm my nerves or I'm going to fucking lose it. I try to keep my thumper to a simmer by reminding myself to *breathe, Max, you're safe inside the Beast.*

The car beside me honks an SOS distress signal. I turn to see what's the dilemma—it's merely a horn-happy boomer dressed in a navy pinstripe suit, sipping a white coffee cup inside his cream 550 SL. He's trying to break into my lane. Our eyes lock, I shrug, then he gives me the middle finger, mouthing obscenities too wicked for me to repeat.

As if that's how to get your way? I hate to break it to you, Mr. Pinstripe, but it's bumper-to-bumper traffic, so do us all a favor, lay off the bean juice and fucking relax.

Mr. Pinstripe doesn't chill. His road rage persists and spreads throughout the auto grid faster than a summer wildfire in strong wind. People shout, honk, and try to weave in and out of backed-up lanes. The noise becomes as hair-curling painful as an off-off-Broadway opera. I swear on my mother's soul that white cup will be the death of me.

My nerves settle when the gridlock eases, allowing me to merge for an upcoming turn. The Beast inches into the next lane but stops short when a speeding Bronco zooms past, missing her beefy bumper by less than a hair, then smashes—BAM!—into the rear of a Whatcom County bus.

The Bronco is sideways on its driver's-side door, and soon both vehicles are on fire; dozens of screaming passengers spill into the streets.

What the fucko is wrong with that Bronco?

And it's not only civilians driving like maniacs this morning. Get this—moments earlier, pre-gridlock, I'm driving the Beast down Alabama Hill when I catch my mail carrier Tanya moving at highway speeds. She cuts me off then swerves around a Volvo. Her mail truck's tires smoke as she skids sideways, missing a head-on collision with a church van stuffed with blue-haired believers, and fishtails once, twice—

KAA-BOOM!

She takes out a multi-residential mailbox. The letter boxes explode into shrapnel, leaving a mushroom cloud of junk mail like New Year's confetti. I'm burning up, sweating, watching from the comforts of my—

Damn.

I almost forgot ... the Beast. How could I be so inconsiderate as to not give her the proper introduction that she deserves?

I purchased my black Chevrolet Suburban eight years ago at a state auction for a ridiculous price because her electronics are fried, she's missing her back seats, and she's got nine hundred thousand miles clocked on her odometer. Plus, as much as I hate to say it, the Beast isn't easy on the eyes; she has a crapload of dents and scrapes.

Why bother with a beat-up car with close to a million miles, you ask?

I crunched the numbers. It's a hell of a lot cheaper and environmentally greener to take care of the vehicle you own instead of replacing it with something glittery-new. But the main reason is that the Beast, pound per dollar, is my best bet for surviving an accident. Go ahead and snicker all you want, but the fact is that last year alone, 2.7 million people in the US were injured or killed in an auto accident.

That's how I lost my father. He was only thirty-two when he got T-boned in his lime-green Chevy Chevette by a chickenshit hit-and-run driver. It happened late on some bumfuck nowhere road.

The Beast is worth it for my peace of mind. She's burly and she keeps me at ease. I've kept up with her maintenance and her V8 is solid. I love the Beast, but if I'm going to be honest with you, the single issue I have with her is that she's a thirsty girl, six miles per gallon going downhill thirsty. Right now, her stomach is growling, near empty.

HONK!

As if being an asshole were contagious, another dickhead driver beside me lays down hard on his horn. After several nerve-shredding moments, I look toward the prick with my hands up, shrugging as if to say: *What the hell do you want?*

His honking doesn't stop, but that's okay because beyond the noisy prick, I've spotted my freedom, my escape out of this hell.

There's an alleyway kitty-corner from me, and if my memory serves me, this non-Google-mapped passage will guide me to a gas station where I can fill her up for cheap as long as I pay with cash. I draw my wallet from the ass pocket of my jeans and peek behind my driver's license. Bingo. There's my emergency Benjamin, right where I left him.

The logjam loosens and there's a traffic gap. I punch through it then beeline toward the best-priced gas station in town. Unfortunately, when I arrive there's a line of motorists wrapped around the pump, spewing into the street. If I stick around, I'll be late for work and most likely run out of fuel waiting in line, so I nix the gas idea. I can coast down the remaining blocks if I can make it to Holly.

The Beast shakes but doesn't die as we climb up to Holly Street and turn. From the road's peak, you can see a chunk of the eighty-thousand-plus Bellingham residents' homes, the cool steel blue of Bellingham Bay, the majestic San Juan Islands, and the historic buildings that make up most of downtown.

On a clear day, not today, you can see an old brick building nestled close to the docks. That's me—my salvation, my clinic Brighter Days, on the ground floor in a south-facing unit.

I shift the Beast into neutral to coast down Holly, and I realize unlike uptown, downtown Bellingham is vacant and pin-drop quiet. There aren't any buses, cyclists, cars, or pedestrians in any direction, and the sudden contrast sticks me with a sickening feeling that I can't shake.

This morning's commute has me bent out of shape. I'm a fucking wreck and my gut aches, as empty as the Beast. A gnawing hunger overwhelms me, clouding out all reason. I glance down at the dashboard clock and it's eleven minutes before noon. I have time for a treat. Hell, I *deserve* a treat. Fortunately for me, Larry's Donut Shop is just up ahead. But when I pull up to the curb, I discover that the shop's windows are boarded up with plywood. Red paint across the boards announces: CLOSED.

Closed on Friday before noon?

I study the streets for anything open, but all the storefronts are dark except one. At the bottom of Holly, I spot a twinkle of hope—the familiar glow of an orange marquee belonging to the Horseshoe, Bellingham's famous twenty-four-hour diner, the best late-night spot for food and gossip.

I shift the Beast into drive and step on her accelerator; screw the gas. Once I'm close, I stuff her gear into park, jump out, and jog toward the doors. My glands salivate as I daydream of fluffy flapjacks piled high with whipped cream on top. Those hopes deflate when I notice that the Horseshoe's doors are padlocked shut. A message across the window reads: SAVE YOURSELVES.

I shove my face against the glass door. Inside,

the lights are off, but I can still see that the tables are flipped over and there's broken dishes flung across the diner's floor. The place has been ransacked. What the hell?

"You there!" shouts a rough voice.

A pack of gutter punks is across the street. They've concealed their faces with hoods and masks, and they're clothed in black leather and denim like some Mad Max gang ready for battle, swinging chains above their heads, spiked wooden bats resting on their shoulders.

The tallest punk in the pack points his leather-gloved finger at me, his other hand tugging a bandana down from his mouth. He yells, "Get your ass over here!"

I mimic his gesture, pointing my finger at my chest as I ask in a falsetto voice, "Who, me?"

He nods, but I don't comply. Time slows. I count the heartbeats inside my chest. Two, three, four, heartbeats later, the pack races at me like wild animals on the Discovery channel. My muscles tense and I freeze, staring at the stampede running in slow motion with their fists pumping, boots stomping, and one purple-haired banshee screeching at the top of her lungs.

I count five, six, seven heartbeats, then a voice inside my head screams: *RUN!*

Now moving in real-time, I book it toward the Beast, running as fast as humanly possible toward safety. I make it inside the cab and lock her up, but I can't take off—the punks swarm the Beast like bees on summer tea. They begin beating her with chains, bats, and fists.

"Get off her, you bastards!" I scream. I slump into my worn leather seat, paralyzed as they rock my ride back and forth, as psychotic as soccer fans after the World Cup. All around me are horrid sounds of scraping metal and heels thumping against glass. I'd piss myself if my bladder were full. The voice screams again: *DRIVE!*

I slam the pedal to metal. The Beast's knobby tires run over boot-covered feet as she surges into the street, and I check my rearview mirror until the punks are nothing but specks of dust in the reflection. What the fuck is going on around here? All I know is that it's minutes before noon and if I hurry, I'll have time for a quick fix.

2. Warm and fuzzy

Once inside my clinic, I lock up and head straight toward Booth #1, shove myself inside the snug, windowless room, and undress until I'm barefoot in my briefs. I press a START button on the wall, and a semi-circle of magenta LED light erupts from the booth. My skin tingles from the pleasant warmth of my fine-tuned machine as it blankets me with magenta lightwaves. In this cozy haven, all my stress and hunger melt away like butter on a hot pan.

I didn't want to mention it earlier, but now, seeing that I'm feeling much better, I'll tell you what I usually keep to myself: I'm absolutely terrified of death. Merely hearing the word *death* leaves me like an acrophobic leaning over the Grand Canyon. I'll get lightheaded and drop to the floor, trembling uncontrollably. *Death*. The thought of my body spending an eternity underground cripples me, and the thought of my consciousness ending brings on a full panic attack. Thanatophobia is the medical diagnosis, and it's haunted me since I was seven, which is way too young to have such an extreme phobia weighing down a developing mind.

The fear first surfaced at my grandfather's funeral. I remember it as if it happened last week. I stood beside my parents in a long line of relatives and friends, waiting for our moment to say our goodbyes. It was my first funeral, and I didn't understand anything about death. I asked my mother why this had to happen to Grandpa. My mother's never had much of a filter, even toward children. She kneeled toward me and whispered, "You know Max, this will be you, me, and your father one day. We're *all* going to die, sweetie. Everyone will end up six feet underground. There's nothing we can do to change a thing about it."

Heavy, I know, but her bluntness wasn't meant to hurt me. My mother is who she's always been, matter-of-fact. She didn't know that what she said that day would stick with me forever. Her words popped my childlike bubble of a world where until that morning, I thought I would live forever. That same day, I believed in Santa and the Easter Bunny. I thought I could live on

Sesame Street one day. The startling new information looped inside my brain as I walked toward my grandfather's casket.

This will be me.

We're all going to die.

On my tippy toes, I ogled my grandfather's dull gray face as my mother's words repeated over and over again. *Me, him, her, everyone will end up six feet underground. There's nothing you can do about it. Me, him, her …*

I remember a rush of blistering heat running through me. A suffocating weight on my chest. I couldn't breathe. I felt my body sinking to the ground, the world went black, and I woke up in a hospital bed hours later.

Near my ninth birthday, I attended two more funerals where I fainted at each—once at my cousin's, then three months later at my father's. Mother reminded me: *me, him, her, everyone …*

My thanatophobia worsened as time passed, and the fear of death came to interfere with my day-to-day life. I became an anxious, paranoid mess of a child. Then in sixth grade, my teacher Miss Robinson reached out to my mother. She insisted we seek professional help.

My mother took me to see my general practitioner. After we chatted, he strongly suggested I see a children's shrink.

When I met with the psychiatrist, whose

name I can't remember, she reassured me that the fear of death is quite common, especially among kids who have lost family at a young age. At the end of our session, she sent me away with a prescription slip. In her professional opinion, mind-numbing pills were the answer.

The capsules prescribed did, in fact, mute my worries. Those purple pills did a great job of masking paranoid thoughts and replacing them with warm and fuzzy sensations, smiley faces, and happy trees.

But when the medication wore off, it left me feeling lethargic and disconnected from the world, my mind dull and foggy. Then the anxiety would seep back in like a nightmare gradually taking over a dream, and to escape the horror of my thoughts, I would swallow another handful of purple pills, and repeat.

It was awful existing out-of-my-mind high, or sluggish, or as an absolute nervous wreck, so after three years—which I swear to this day felt like twice that—I stopped taking the drugs cold turkey. I was determined to get my life back on track.

Many painful years later, I can confidently say that I'm functioning. I found an alternative therapeutic regimen to the pills. Around two years ago, my search engine's algorithm suggested I try light therapy. An online ad linked me to a clinic in Seattle; I made an appointment, drove a hundred miles south, and became a believer after my initial session. Light therapy became my savior. Not only can my pale skin enjoy the warm magenta light that mimics the sun's rays without burning, the lights boost serotonin in the brain, which leaves me with a feeling of euphoria for hours.

For a while I made daily trips to Seattle. Eventually I picked up a booth for myself. The therapy shook me back to life—for the first time in my adulthood, I felt motivated, capable, energized. I felt impelled to share this revolutionary experience with others, so I spent the last penny to my name, plus a bank loan, to build the first and only light therapy clinic in Whatcom County.

After a year, my clinic is doing okay. I still have bank bills to pay back, so I work here alone seven days a week. I'm not raking it in, but my head's above water. It helps that business has picked up since the end of summer. Here in the upper Pacific Northwest, it's common for the sun to disappear for most of the year, leaving a lot of folks with seasonal depression. Light therapy helps curb those winter blues.

And for me, I get access to as much medical light as I want. In fact, I haven't gone a day without a light fix since I started using, and frankly, I don't want to find out what would happen if I quit now.

DING DONG!

My eyelids burst open. It must be my twelve-fifteen appointment. I button my shirt, kill the lights, and make my way toward the front. The doorbell ringing is replaced by furious pounding against the door.

BAM! BAM!

Customers sometimes show up early and agitated, but I don't sweat it. I get it. They need a zap, and it's my job to provide them with what they need.

BAM! BAM! BAM!

Jeez, hold up, I'm coming.

"Max! Come on, man, hurry up and open the damn door!"

"Carter?" I ask, my face close to the door.

"Yes! Now, let me in!"

I twist the deadbolt and my old friend Carter barrels in, spinning in circles like a cartoon Tasmanian devil. He stops, then cries, "Lock it!"

"What?"

Carter rushes to the door and shuts it, twisting the deadbolt in place. "Don't let anyone inside!"

Carter isn't in his usual pseudo-gym attire of basketball shorts and tank tops that never match. If it weren't for his familiar deep and resonant voice, I would have mistaken him for one of those gutter punks at first glance. He's in black threads from head to toe, with a beanie covering his Bicbald dome and an army-green backpack slung over his shoulders.

"Why shouldn't I let anyone in?" I ask, approaching him. He's always been a bit paranoid, but he's never acted this strange before.

Carter's eyebrows shoot up. "Haven't you heard?"

"Heard what?"

"Do you feel sick?" He backs away from me.

"I'm fine. What the hell is wrong with you?"

"Nothing's wrong with *me*," Carter says, curling his hands into fists. "Just fine, huh? Do you have a fever?" He takes another wary step back.

"No! What's gotten into you?" I snap.

Carter shoves his smartphone into my face. "Here, look for yourself."

There's a video titled *Washington State Emergency*. Two news anchors are sitting behind a studio desk, repeating: "Phase Zero emergency lockdown goes into effect at six o' clock tonight for all Washington residents. This is not a drill. Phase Zero—"

I smack his phone away. "What the fuck was that? Are you messing with me again with this *War of the Worlds* shit?"

Carter shakes his head. "Dude, I wish this was fake news. Something huge is going down right now."

I rip my phone from my pocket and launch

YouTube. At the top of my feed are today's trending clips. I tap play on a video titled *Rampage in Emerald City*.

The video comprises monochromatic security camera footage cut with shaky phone video clips of adults losing their minds inside a big-box department store. People running through near-empty aisles, grabbing whatever food or supplies they can fit into their shopping carts: canned goods, vitamins, water, booze, tampons, paper products. The video cuts to a close-up shot of two men fist-fighting over a case of soda, then cuts to women pulling hair over frozen TV dinners and others wrestling over bags of dog food. I can't believe what I'm seeing.

Hands on his hips and head tilted up to the ceiling, Carter paces and mutters profanity. I've never seen him so tense.

The next video is titled *Chaos In The Streets*. I press play. It opens with a drone shot of the Space Needle in Seattle. The flying camera pulls back from the iconic structure, exposing nearby multi-storied towers billowing with smoke, then cuts to close-ups of boarded-up businesses, then to body camera footage from a police officer's point of view pushing back a crowd of pissed-off protesters. The body camera cuts to a cop hog-tying a young woman, then to a crowd running from tear gas and bean bags.

"This is the end!" Carter yells. "It's all happening now!"

New videos appear in my feed, each one supplanted by the next. I feel lightheaded. I sink down on a chair and watch video after video of the entire state going apeshit insane.

Breaking news: HIT is spreading throughout Washington State.

Breaking news: Thousands have died.

Breaking news: Hospitals are out of beds.

Breaking news: Flights are canceled in and out of all Washington airports.

Breaking news: All schools are closed until further notice.

Breaking news: Washington State borders are sealed shut.

Breaking news: Riots are erupting into the streets.

Breaking news: Statewide lockdown starting tonight at six.

I can't comprehend what I'm seeing. I take a deep breath before clicking another video, this one captioned *Washington Medical Emergency: HIT*.

An elderly doctor wearing a hazmat suit with the hood down stands in the middle of a crowded hospital hallway. He looks into the camera lens and speaks.

"Greetings, my name is Dr. Howson. My team and I recently identified a highly contagious pathogen spreading through the state of Washington at alarming speeds. We call it—" he mumbles some long, scientific-sounding jargon, "—or for short, HIT. As of now, all we understand of HIT is that it spreads through human touch. Once caught, HIT will compromise vital organs. It was first discovered in Seattle, and by now, there have been thousands of cases reported in and around the city, many of them leading to deaths. Early symptoms of HIT include high fever, loss of appetite, fatigue, diarrhea, and vomiting blood. I urge all residents to isolate yourselves from one another until we can slow the spread."

Dr. Howson's message causes my hands to shake. His words repeat in my head. *Deaths, loss of appetite, vomiting blood.*

I'm queasy. Do I have HIT? I need a moment to get my bearings straight—what I need is another fix. I rush inside Booth #4 and rip off my clothes. I slam on the machine and soak in the calming rays. I try my best to let the light transport me far away to a mellow oasis, a news-free island in the sun. But his words make their way back inside my brain. *Thousands of cases.*

I can't shut the doctor up. I have to find out what the fuck else is going on, so I pull out my phone again and press play.

In the magenta light, I watch the latest trending video on my feed, titled *Phase Zero*. The clip begins with Washington State Governor Louise Holtz entering stage right, waving her hands like a prom queen floating down Main Street in a Fourth of July parade. Her arms fall to her side once she's behind a podium stamped with the state's seal. Behind the governor are her family members, Mr. Holtz and their children whose names I don't recall, twin boys and a little girl.

Governor Holtz clears her throat then speaks into the mic. "As your governor, it's my sworn duty to keep my citizens safe from all threats within our borders, whether foreign, domestic, or epidemic. Today, I stand before you to tell you that we have a deadly enemy among us named HIT."

The camera angle tightens on the governor's face. "Protection against HIT is now priority number one. To control its spread, a new lockdown protocol called Phase Zero will begin tonight at six. During Phase Zero, leaving your home at any time without clearance is forbidden. Public gatherings are prohibited. Business operations will stop unless deemed essential. While you and your families are safely quarantined at home, my team will have trucks working around the clock to deliver goods to households. Fellow Washingtonians, if we work together by following official lockdown procedures, we will soon eliminate HIT and keep our loved ones safe. Thank you for your trust in me. Goodni—"

"Max!"

It's Carter. I turn off the light booth, pocket my phone, dress, and rejoin him in the lobby. He asks, "Do you understand now?"

"Yeah. I guess so ... Shit."

"*Shit* is right. Max, I'm so glad you're here because I have a—"

RING!

Carter's phone. He answers. "Pops. What? No. I'm fine. No. Don't do that. I'll be over soon with your—"

He wanders into a light booth, still talking. I realize that I need to call my mother.

A pleasant-sounding woman answers my call. "Thanks for calling King County Care. Jane speaking. How can I assist you today?"

"Hi, this is Max Maddison. I'm calling for my mother, Anne Maddison, room 308. Can you transfer me, please?"

"Sure, Mr. Maddison, hold on while I direct your call." Recorded ambient sounds of waterfalls fill my ear. How can she sound so calm? King County Care is less than twenty miles north of Seattle, ground zero. For fuck's sake Mom, pick up your damn phone!

"Yes, who is it?" She sounds tired, as if she just woke up.

"It's Max."

"Who?"

"It's your one and only son, Max. Are you feeling alright?"

"Do ... I feel ... alright?"

"Do you have a fever? Loss of appetite? Any bloody vomit, or diarrhea?"

"Diarrhea? Honey, I'm fine. Are you okay? Are you off your med—"

Bzzzzzz. Then icy silence. My phone battery just died. Damnit.

Carter reappears as I'm fumbling with my dead phone. Twisting the dark whiskers on his chin, he says, "Max, we need to get out of here and gather supplies before this lockdown shit hits the fan."

I stop messing with my phone and direct my attention toward Carter. "Where would we go? All the stores must be empty by now—"

"I'm not talking retail, man. I'm thinking wholesale."

"What?"

"Nevermind. Did you drive here?"

"Didn't you see the Beast out front? Why?"

"We'll need her to help us."

"Help us with what?"

"Supplies, man. Now get us the hell out of here and drive us north!"

"Hold up. I can't just leave. I have bookings all after—"

"What bookings? We're in quarantine. And if we don't get going soon, we'll have bigger problems."

BANG! BANG!

Gunshots ring outside. We drop to the floor, hearing car tires outside burn rubber followed by human screams. I'm trembling and my heart feels like it's going to explode from my chest. We remain flat on our bellies until the commotion outside fades. Carter whips his face toward me. "Can we go now?"

He's right. It's not safe. Downtown is a complete shitstorm and we're in the eye of it.

3. Some kind of prank

On bone-chilling days like today, I don't speed off into the street until the Beast is warm with her RPM needle hovering a pinch over one thousand. My father implemented this regimen into me. He had owned that '77 Chevette his entire life and would swear up and down that allowing time for the engine to warm up was the single reason his wheels kept moving for all those years.

"She needs a minute," I explain to Carter while wiping condensation off the windshield with the back of my flannel sleeve.

"We don't have a minute. We gotta get going now."

"Too bad. The Beast is cold, and I don't drive until she's—"

SCREEEEECH! BAM!

Up ahead at the intersection of Bay Street, a candy-apple-red Firebird and a silver three-series BMW have obliterated themselves in a head-on collision, scattering glass and plastic all over the road.

"Shitballs," Carter mumbles under his breath.

I calculate mathematics in my head. At sixty miles per hour, you're traveling eighty-eight feet per second. If two cars pounded each other head-on at that speed, the impact would feel like you were going 120. The survival rate is less than one percent.

"C'mon! Let's go!" Carter yells, distracting me from my death equation. I glance at the Beast's tachometer.

"Not yet. She needs to warm up."

"Oh, donkey balls. Who told you that nonsense?"

"My fa—"

KA-BOOM!

I'm cut short by a blast so violent that its shock waves shake the Beast. A fireball erupts from the wreckage, billowing purple smoke into the gray sky. The cars have exploded, guaranteeing an absolute zero chance of survival. They're goners and I hope they died from the initial head-on collision because I've read that it doesn't get much worse than being burned alive.

"Fuck me," Carter says.

Fuck me is right.

They're dead and will end up six feet deep underground in a box. Underground. That's where I'm going in the end, me, them, everyone—

"Hey," Carter says, slapping my shoulder. "Can we fucking go now?"

I ignore him as I stare into the raging fire, waiting, hoping for someone to crawl from the remains, but nothing. The fire roars, its smoke growing thicker with every passing second. I turn to Carter. "Shouldn't we call 911?"

"No way. No one can help them now."

"Yeah, but what if the fire spreads?"

I yank my phone from my jeans pocket and press the power button, but a drained battery image flashes on the screen. *Shit*. I can't charge it. Not here. The Beast lacks modern luxuries, like a working 9-volt input or USB. Nobody's perfect.

"You gotta make the call. My phone's dead."

Carter crosses his arms. "I don't want to call the police and end up in their system."

"You won't if you star-sixty-seven the call."

"That shit doesn't work."

"Yes it does."

"Well, I don't want my voice recorded either."

"So we just leave them there, burning like that?"

Carter lets out an agitated exhale.

"Fine, you can use my phone, but you have to do all the talking."

Carter dials 911 and puts his phone on speaker. It rings twice, then a robotic voice message begins. "Thanks for calling your local Whatcom County emergency center. We're experiencing higher-than-usual call volume at this moment. Your estimated speaking time with an emergency operator is two minutes."

Soft elevator music suffocates the cab.

"We're on hold. With 911. Is that even *legal*?" I ask.

Carter shakes his head. "I'm not so sure what *legal* even means anymore."

A New York minute passes, then a fast-talking operator answers our call. "911, what's your emergency?"

I clear my throat. "Yes, hello. I'm calling to report that there's been an accident."

I hear the operator's fingers tapping on her keyboard. "What kind of accident, sir? You'll have to be specific."

"A car accident. Two cars, head-on collision, and now there's a fire. You gotta send someone quick—"

"Sir, we cannot help you. You'll need to call a tow truck for automobile accidents."

"What? This is an emergency, so I thought—"

"Sir, please understand Phase Zero emergency protocol's number one priority is the control of HIT. Emergency personnel cannot assist with accidents that aren't related to HIT. So unless this call is—"

"This shit is bonkers!" Carter yells.

"What was that, sir?" the operator asks.

I punch Carter in the arm and jerk his phone close to my mouth.

The operator continues, "If this is some kind of prank, you'll have bigger problems."

"No. N-No, ma'am," I stutter. "That was nothing. Umm, so let me get this straight. You will do nothing, and I should call a tow truck?"

"Yes, sir. I have your car accident report noted here and—"

Carter shakes his head, grabs his phone, and hangs up.

"Max, I told you. This goddamn state has gone batshit and nobody is going to help us. It's just you, me, and—"

BANG BANG!

Bullets graze the Beast's shell.

"Step on it!" Carter screams.

I slam her into drive and give her gas. The Beast takes off like a rocket. We pass the flaming wreckage and race through the remaining downtown blocks.

Carter yells, "Hang a Roger here!"

Without letting off the gas, I yank the wheel

and all four tires skid across the pavement, narrowly missing a light post.

"Nice one, Andretti. Now, at that light, take a left and—"

BZZZZZZZZZ! The Beast shakes, then her power steering stiffens. We lose power and coast to a stop at the edge of downtown.

"What the fuck happened?" Carter asks.

The gas needle is below empty. "We're out of gas."

Carter smacks the dash and mutters, "Well ... shit." Then he brightens and points ahead. "Over there. That neon light at the end of the block is a gas station. Let's push and—"

BANG BANG!

More gunshots. I duck down in my seat. "I'll stay inside the comforts of the Beast, thank you very much."

"What then? You sit around and wait for fucking triple-A to come help by next Tuesday?"

"Yeah. I have blankets plus a water jug and—"

"No fucking way, Max. We don't have time for that shit. Let me take the rear and all you have to do is steer. Let's go. Clock's ticking." Carter jumps out and heads toward the rear bumper.

Fuck. I drop her into neutral then hop out, keeping one hand steady on the wheel with the other gripping the door. Standing in the street, I feel vulnerable, like I have a target on my back.

"Are you ready up there?" Carter asks.

"I guess so."

"On three, we push. Got it?"

"Yeah. On three."

"Okay. One, two, three, push."

We huff and puff. I hear Carter grunting between breaths. I'm losing strength and tempted to call it quits, but then the Beast begins to inch forward.

"That's it, keep it going!" Carter hollers with glee.

We're closing in on the gas station. It can't be more than a frisbee toss away. I give her another push, and another. She's moving. Suddenly the wind picks up and a freezing gale tears through me. I turn to shield myself against the Beast's door and look back toward Carter to see that he's now running at me with his body glowing, backlit by bright lights.

"Get out of the way!" Carter yells. He grabs my wrist and yanks me away from the Beast.

CRUNCH!

4. Get some

I fall on my funny bone. Where I was just standing, now there's a Cadillac with its front smashed. The Caddy's hood is bent to hell, utterly destroyed, and my beloved Beast is ghost-riding down the street, weaving like a drunkard. Before I can get up, she slams into a tall curb.

My muscles tighten up and my blood boils. All I see is red, and then, like a pissed-off parent at a Little League T-ball game over a missed foul, I fucking lose it. I scramble to my feet and charge toward the driver's-side door, shouting, "What the hell you sonofabitch-fuckface-moron—"

I stop when I notice that the Caddy airbags have gone off and the driver appears to be unconscious. Is that blood I see dripping from his ear? My nostrils flare at an acrid smell like paint thinner.

"It's on fire!" Carter yells.

Smoke fills the cab. I pull on the door handle, but it's stuck.

"It's gonna blow," Carter warns. "Fucking get away."

We run.

KA-BOOM!

The Cadillac explodes, sending Carter and me into the air. I'm on the ground again, shell-shocked. I hear pitter-patter sounds all around me. Hail?

Smoldering hunks of metal and plastic rain from the sky. A bent chrome fender skips past me like a desert tumbleweed. The Cadillac's iconic wreath emblem lands beside my boot. The driver is a goner, and this time, I don't suggest calling 911.

I haul ass toward my Beast. Her damage seems minimal—a fist-sized dent above her rear plate. That's my baby, sturdy as hell.

Carter approaches me and asks, "Is she gonna be okay?"

"I think so."

"She is one tough-ass ride." Carter runs his hand affectionately across the Beast's side, then he jabs one finger down the street. "Max, that's us, fuel for your Beast. How about it? One big push and—"

"Hell no, we won't go! No Phase Zero!"

Behind us at the end of the block, a crowd of protesters marches into view with picket signs. I blink and they're swarmed by deputies, wielding batons and shooting tear gas canisters. The protesters scream and scatter, and Carter and I duck behind the Beast.

I ram my palms against her bumper and look at Carter. "What are we waiting for?"

Carter calls out, "One, two, three, push!" We thrust our weights forward. Carter's spine bends like a drawn bow. I hurl all my one hundred and fifty pounds against the Beast. She inches forward.

"Keep ... it ... going," Carter pants.

With one more big push, the Beast's tires roll.

"Grab ... the ... wheel," Carter commands.

I leave my post, jump behind the wheel, and wrench her tires toward the gas station. The Beast gains momentum. I steer her alongside a pump, put her in park, and jump out.

Carter runs up and rests his hands on his beanie-covered dome as he struggles to catch his breath. I poke my head around for a gas attendant, but nobody's home.

"How do I pre-pay around here?"

"You don't," Carter replies. He walks toward the pump and taps his finger against an engraved plaque. It reads: AUTHORIZED COMMERCIAL CREDIT CARDS ONLY. "This is a commercial pump stop. You know, big-wheelers, truck drivers."

"You realize I'm not a trucker, right?"

"Maybe you aren't," Carter says, tugging his wallet from his jeans pocket, "but Pops is."

He shoves a glossy credit card in my face. There's a golden horse's head logo, and beneath that, embossed letters spell out: TEAMSTERS OF AMERICA. Carter slides the plastic through the card reader.

"I don't remember Chuck driving a big rig."

Carter pushes buttons on the keypad, and the card reader beeps. The word AUTHORIZED appears on the monochromatic screen.

"He was a Teamster for years in California, you know, movie stuff, before we moved up here."

"I must have forgotten."

"Nah, I probably never mentioned it. It was a long time ago, but his perks still work. Premium?"

I nod. Carter smacks the 93-octane button. I remove the gas cap, and he inserts the nozzle into the fuel filler.

I hand my emergency hundo to Carter. "Here, cash for the gas."

"On the house."

I shove the bill closer to him. "It will cost at least this to fill her. Take it."

He waves away my offering. "Max, don't worry about it."

"Well, give it to Chuck then."

"Pops wouldn't want your cash either."

"Why not?"

"For starters, that hundred won't be worth anything by next week."

"What are you talking about?"

Carter straightens and looks intently at me. "Let me put it to you like this. Would you eat that hundred-dollar bill?"

"What kind of question is that?"

"A realistic one."

"You're ridiculous."

"Okay. Different question, would you wipe your ass with that hundred?"

I cock my head to the side. "You're kidding me. What are you getting at?"

Carter shakes his head. "Max. Forget about cash. What we need are essential supplies, because without them, life from here on out will suck ass ten times more than it already has."

"What supplies are you talking about? Canned food, water, what?"

"Food is easy. If I have to, I'll walk into the forest and shoot myself dinner. And water? Please, there's enough in Lake Whatcom to last us for years. No, dude, what I'm after is the *only* thing that matters after the fact."

"After what fact?"

"You tell me. You watched the videos, right?

People running around in empty stores looting whatever they can get their dirty hands on."

"Sure. How could I forget?"

"Well, what I'm after is the stuff you need *after* you've stuffed yourself with boxed macaroni, canned ravioli, and fucking frozen burrito crap. Max, we need toilet paper."

I take a moment, waiting to see if he's going to slap me across my back and tell me *gotcha*, but Carter remains still. He's serious.

"What? You're telling me that with everything that's going on, of all the things we could be stockpiling, what we need right now is toilet paper?"

"Yes. And I know a mother lode. But the thing is, it's in this warehouse that's a serious trek and a half away, so I'll need you to drive your Beast and we'll load her up with the ass-wipe. So if we leave—"

"Hold up for just a second and let's think about this. We're going to break into a warehouse and then fill the Beast with ... toilet paper? Tonight?"

"Yeah."

"And we're going to do this because you think cash is going to be worthless, so toilet paper will become, what? Currency?"

"Exactly."

My shoulders sag. "Carter, I'm beat, so here,

please, just take my hundred and I'll take you wherever—"

Carter doesn't let up. If anything, he gets more agitated. "Max, I don't want your cash. I don't think you understand the severity of our situation. Grocery stores won't replenish with supplies. This Zero shit gives our governor complete control over all the supply chains, and I don't know about you, but I don't like the sound of that for a fucking second. Phase Zero is just another word for martial law. Complete control over us citizens. Wake up! This is some fucking 1984 shit."

"Christ ... I get it, but what if this disease, this HIT-thing, goes away? You know, scientists find a cure and the state returns to normalcy in a few weeks. Is it worth breaking and entering for some stupid toilet paper?"

"Yes, it is worth it, Max. Don't you get it? The Governor and her Phase Zero shit, it's all too orchestrated."

"It's her job to be ready when things like this happen."

"Right. You're telling me she has already lined up enough trucks to ship goods for millions of residents? It's shit, man. Stinks if you ask me. Tell me, why don't the other forty-nine states seal their borders? Or demand that their residents stay indoors indefinitely? Or even help us out?"

"I'm not sure, but—"

"I don't know about you, Max. I'm not gonna sit around with my thumb up my ass to wait for a fucking truck to drop off a limited supply of government cheese. Max, listen to me. Nothing will go back to normal. This is the new normal. This lockdown is going to get fucking worse, and nobody is going to help us, okay? I will not wait for a handout or wait for change. I will take what's mine while I still have the chance!"

The pump stops fueling. Carter sets the nozzle back into its holster. "Max, if you help me with this, I'll cut you half of whatever we get out of it, and I swear you'll get a shit-ton more value off this than that hundred-dollar bill you're flappin'."

"Carter, listen man, I don't want a repeat of that fiasco you talked me into at the Elliott Bay apartments. Remember? Seattle, four years ago."

"You don't need to worry this time," Carter assures me. "It's not trespassing if the place you're entering is nonoperational."

I shake my head. "I don't think that's how the law works. Either way, we can't be out past six. Phase Zero starts tonight, and—"

"If we leave now, we'll have plenty of time before six. I promise."

A full-size RAM truck roars past us on the road at reckless speeds. It swerves, the driver honking like a madman, his arm out the window shooting bullets out into the sky. Tension. Chaos. Pressure. I feel it oozing into the streets, growing stronger, more lethal by the minute.

Carter puts a hand on my shoulder. "Brother, I'm gonna need your help, but you have to tell me right now. There's no going back once we've started. Are you in, or are you out?"

Brother.

It's been years since Carter has called me *brother*. Not since we used to spend every day together like real brothers, but that was years ago, and now I can't tell if he's trying to wheedle his way into my heart with a word he knows can penetrate deep. *Brother.*

I have to admit it though—he came straight to me, and he's standing by me like a brother when the entire state has gone loony. Who else have I got? Fuck.

"Okay ... I'm in."

"Hell yeah, Max. Now let's go get some before it's gone."

5. Vehicular Suicide

We reach the interstate with the Beast's belly chock-full of fuel. I stomp the pedal and give her all the gas she can swallow, and I feel the rumble of her eight cylinders pumping, her engine roaring like a wild animal. Listening to her throaty exhaust is sweet music to my ears as we cruise at seventy-three miles per hour, heading northbound. As I watch the fiery chaos of downtown fading away through the rearview mirror, I feel my jaws unclench.

Carter checks his phone's GPS. "In seven miles, take exit 274," he tells me.

I re-grip the wheel, my hands positioned at ten and two and her RPMs pinned at 2600, the sweet spot. The Beast likes it and so do I. With three tons of reinforced metal surrounding me from the outside world, I can breathe again. Like I said, the

Beast keeps my nerves at a simmer. Right now, I'll take any source of soothing available.

Tension. Chaos. Pressure. My mind drifts as we cruise north on the interstate. I see myself as a kid sitting in my childhood room, winding up my favorite toy, Mr. Jack-in-the-Box. Watching myself twisting the toy's lever, I can feel the spring building pressure. I was well aware a toy Jack was about to pop out and give me a good jump scare, without fail, every time. Yet, I keep winding the toy because the result is enjoyable, predictable. But unlike a toy, if you force pressure on people, it's impossible to predict precisely how a population will pop out of their boxes.

A passing car lifts me from my reminiscing, and I glance over at Carter, who's staring into his phone's bright screen. I tell him, "I never thanked you for saving me back there. Another ten minutes at my clinic, and I don't think I would have made it out of downtown in one piece."

Carter looks up, shrugs, and says, "I got your back, Max."

I think about how long it's been since we've spoken. It's been months. Carter used to come by the clinic all the time. Hell, he helped me with some of the initial setup. Since then, he moved in with his father who lives thirty minutes from Bellingham and rarely makes it down here these days. We fell out of touch.

"Hey, Carter, what were you doing downtown anyway?"

Carter sets his glowing screen on his lap and surveys the two lanes of highway ahead. "I was on my way to pick up a prescription for Pops when my Subaru seized up. So I ditched the stupid car and hoofed it to the pharmacy, but when I arrived, they sealed the doors and then these punks chased me for blocks, and that's when I saw you ..."

Carter trails off and it's quiet for a moment. We add another mile to the odometer.

"How's Chuck these days?" I ask.

Carter falls back into the passenger seat, arms crossed. "Pops? Honestly ... not so great. It's his liver. He needs a transplant like now, but there's a shortage."

"Are you kidding me?"

"I wish. It's just fucking bad timing with this lockdown shit going on. Whatever. *C'est la vie*, right? We'll figure something out. But, hey, enough about Pops, how's your mom? How's Ms. Maddison doing?"

"She's been in a care facility for the last six months or so."

"What for?"

"Early onset dementia."

"Fuck, man. She's so young, what? Mid-forties?"

"Forty-four."

"Damn, Max. That sucks. I hope she's in good hands."

The Beast's headlights illuminate our exit sign 274, and at the end of the off-ramp, we stop at a red traffic light dangling above a three-way intersection.

To the east, amber street lights illuminate a farmhouse, and across from it is a small church. To the west, an empty road disappears into thick woods.

"Which way?" I ask, tapping my fingers on the wheel.

"Let's see." Carter fiddles with his phone. "Give me a second. GPS is offline." He smacks his device against his thigh. "Okay. We need to go ... east."

The light turns green. I twist the wheel and accelerate.

Carter yells, "Wait! Scratch that. We go west."

"Are you sure?" I glance east toward the inviting glow of the street lights.

"I'm positive."

Of course—the barren road. What could possibly go wrong?

We head west. The road transitions into a single dirt lane littered with potholes deep enough to leave you stranded with a flat, and to make matters worse, Mother Nature adds more drama in the form of a storm. Rain unloads on us. The droplets are heavy and sudden, as if the clouds have unzipped their bellies. I set the window wipers to max, keep my eyes glued forward, and focus on the road ahead.

"Stop here!" Carter yells.

I thump the brakes and the Beast slides to an uneven stop on the slick mud. "Where?"

"On my side, behind us."

I reverse, creeping backward until Carter tells me I'm good. Through the sheets of rain, I can barely make out a road branching to the right. We take the dark road, choked by towering trees pressing in from either side. It's almost impossible to see beyond the Beast's hood. The path S-curves then straightens out, and soon after, I stop before a rusted iron gate. The gate is flanked by a concrete wall on both its sides that seems to stretch infinitely, vanishing into fog.

"Drive us closer," Carter says, leaning at the edge of his seat.

I advance the Beast forward until her bumper is inches from the thick bars. My eyes follow the vertical iron upward toward the stone-colored sky. "This is the place?"

"Sure is, look." Carter points out a sign that proclaims:

ANDERSON PAPER MILL
AUTHORIZED PERSONNEL ONLY

"So tell me," I say. "How do we get into Fort Knox?"

"You don't think the Beast can blast through it?"

"Are you kidding? That's six-inch iron and a foot of cement. She's burly, but she's not a goddamn tank."

"Convince me."

"What?"

"Try it. Just once, tap the gate, and tell me if it can or can't happen. She's built for this kind of stuff, right?"

"This was your precious little plan? To drive all the way here and try to smash through a gate with my Beast?"

"Well, yeah."

"You're fucking unbelievable."

"No, I'm determined that we follow through with the plan."

"Don't you think the Beast has already been through enough today? She's been shot at, attacked, and hit by a fucking Cadillac."

"Relax, Max. She's fine, right? I think you're underestimating her potential. Hell, your potential too. Now, don't get it twisted, she's one tough ride, but you're not letting her reach greatness."

"Don't push it, man."

"All I'm asking is that you try. Give it a little love-tap and let's see what happens."

I let out a long and exaggerated breath as I re-examine Fort Knox. The cement seems old, possibly damaged, and the iron is rusted, maybe cracked at the welds.

"One time," I tell Carter. I back the Beast from the gate, shift her into drive, then rev the engine. I imagine the Beast's headlights breaking on impact. Her tires explode. Her aluminum block overheats, and we're trapped inside the cab, burning alive.

I shift her back to park. "I can't. It's vehicular suicide."

Carter chuckles to himself, then says calmly, "I thought you were going to surprise me for a second. Hang tight while I find another way in."

6. Snow-covered Hill

Carter leaves me alone to find a different way inside the defunct Anderson Paper Mill, telling me to keep the Beast running and be on the lookout for unusual activity. He promises he'll be back in fifteen minutes, told me to honk the horn three times if I see anything suspicious, then headed down a muddy path along the side of the concrete wall.

So here I am. Sitting inside the Beast, waiting for Carter's return while keeping a lookout, but I haven't seen anything honk-worthy. Frankly, I can't see much of anything. The conditions outside have worsened. The raindrops have ramped up to kidney-bean size, drumming against the Beast's shell.

I have a small confession to make. I've been

stalling. I should be outside looking for the guy because fifteen minutes has long since come and gone. I keep telling myself, *Give him another minute. What's the harm?* But one more minute becomes hours, and now I'm worried. I guess it's time to go.

Keeping the engine running, I exit into the pissing rain and hoof it down the path that Carter took. Immediately I'm drenched to the bone, and at my third or fourth step, a gust of winter wind slaps me in the face. Ouch! Mother Nature's invisible assault stings my bare flesh. My flannel is sticking to my skin, and the denim around my legs is heavy and stiff, and all the fibers of my DNA want me to go back, but I resist the temptation. Instead, I lower my head against the wind and continue my search.

Many steps later the concrete wall ends, and in its place is a steep embankment. Did he fall over? My heart races as I peer down the edge. No Carter, but I spot a tall chain-link fence below.

"Carter!" I stride further alongside the embankment, shouting, "Carter! Where are you?" There's no response.

Just when I'm about to call it quits, my ears perk up to a rattling sound. I follow the noise, leaping over ferns and shrubs until I stand at what appears to be the end of the path.

"Carter, is that you?"

The rattling stops. "Duh. Get down here."

I plant each step down the steep embankment with care, and when I touchdown, I see Carter manipulating a section of the fence with his hands.

"Look," he says. "This piece is about to give way." Carter rattles the chain links. The fence rolls outward like an ocean wave. "Try it," he tells me. I grab a handful of metal links and shake it fiercely. He's right. It's like a rotted tree ready to fall over.

"What do you think? Can you drive through it?" Carter asks.

It's not the fence that has me worried—the Beast could bulldoze through it with ease. It's the steep, rocky approach that gets me. The way down is thirty-plus degrees and littered with jagged rocks, not to mention the storm adding lack of traction to the task at hand.

"Well?" Carter's face folds into a look that transports me to a memory I haven't thought about in years.

I'm fourteen years old with Carter, and we're looking down a snow-covered hill near Mount Baker with plastic sleds under our arms. He drops his sleigh then says, "I'll race you to the bottom!" He takes off down the mountain. I hesitate, and in that moment of hesitation, I've already convinced myself it's too dangerous. I imagine myself crashing, my limbs splayed out like a rag doll, my neck broken, my blood staining the snow scarlet, steaming hot as it pours from my wounds. I can't do it. So I chicken out and end up walking down the mountain, dragging my sled behind me like a sad Peanuts cartoon character. When I catch up with Carter, he's covered with milk-white flakes. He runs toward me, then stops in his tracks when he realizes I'm not similarly crusted in snow. No badge of courage for yours truly. I watch Carter's smile transform into a look of utter disappointment.

The memory fades and I'm back, standing beside Carter at the bottom of the embankment, and he's waiting for my answer. I hesitate and look away across the flat field beyond the fence. There's a fox stalking through the field. I follow it with my eyes as it springs and dives into a shrub. The fox re-emerges and trots off with its dinner grasped in its jaws.

I glance back at Carter. He seems to have missed the entire National Geographic special because all he says is, "Can she plow through this thing or what?"

I give the fence one more tug. It's a baby tooth ready to be pulled with string. I tell Carter to follow me. We climb up the rocky slope, and once we're back inside the Beast, we drive her to the embankment, inch toward the edge, and peer down from our seats. The angle is daunting. There is no way we'll make it down this cliff in one piece. Carter still has that *look* on his face. Fuck it.

"You better buckle up," I tell him as I back up. Once our seatbelts click, I rev the engine. Carter braces himself against the dash. The Beast's tires skid on the mud until they catch. Her engine redlines through the first, second gear, then poof, we're airborne. The cab is quiet as we seem to move in slow motion. I feel weightless as we soar down toward the chain-link fence. I watch the metal links become clearer and larger as we barrel toward it like a goddamn spaceship.

THUD!

The Beast bashes high into an upright fence pole. The impact rattles my ribs. I look out my window. We're losing altitude. Damn you, gravity. I prepare for impact, keeping a tight grip on the wheel.

THUMP!

The Beast topples onto the spongy meadow. Her suspension collapses into the wheel well and I rock back into my seat. Metal scrapes violently underneath; glancing out, I see embers spewing from the undercarriage. I slam my boot down on the brake, and now we're skidding, sliding, and I clench my teeth until the Beast comes to a halt.

Carter rips his hands off the dash. "Max. That was fucking awesome." He slaps my shoulder. "I never thought in a million years you would pull off something like that."

"Are you okay?"

"Okay? I'm fucking great. But what about your Beast?"

I tear open the door and jump out of my seat to investigate. After a thorough examination, I conclude that she's fine. The tires are intact, and the engine isn't smoking. She'll live, but it's the fence that will need reconstructive surgery. The main support poles are bent over, and segments of the corroded chain are scattered throughout the field. I crawl back into my seat to find Carter rubbing his forehead. He says, "Tell me she's okay?"

"She'll live."

Carter nods and says, "Thank goodness." He cracks his neck. "See those buildings?"

I squint at several dim structures in the distance. From here, they're the size of Legos.

"Yeah, I see them."

"That's the mill," Carter explains. "Drive us closer."

I pop the Beast into four-wheel drive then give her some gas, and we bounce inside the cab like bobbleheads over the uneven terrain. I keep her in second gear, a tick under twenty miles per hour, maximizing our traction. Before long, my skull is aching from all the bobbing. I'm thinking we should pause for a break when Carter tells me, "Veer in near that pile of logs."

Up ahead on my left are stacks of lumber piled high as a house, towering over us as we drive closer. The Beast's headlights illuminate our way, exposing neglected industrial structures, silos, ragged and rusted conveyor belts, and terrifying machines bearing outsized Freddy Krueger claws.

Carter leans forward, nose pointing outward like a signaling hunting dog. "Do you see that building with the steel roof? Take us there."

I navigate us through the paper mill's lot, swerving past wooden crates, snapped cable wire, and chunks of cement scattered on the asphalt.

"I had no idea this was here. How do you know about this place?" I ask.

"The mill? My aunt and uncle used to work here until it closed."

"When did it close?"

"It was the summer of '91, or '92, whatever year Clinton won office."

"*Why* did it close?"

Carter lets out a sigh. "I'll give you the Wikipedia version. It's just easier that way." He launches into a monologue.

"In the late 1940s, the Anderson brothers set out to construct the largest paper mill west of the

Mississippi. The brothers knew they needed to secure a discounted electrical rate in order to turn a major profit. So prior to construction, the brothers negotiated with Pacific General Electric, which everyone in this county uses. After long negotiations, PGE agreed on a discounted energy rate, but with a catch: They will void the cheap power contract after forty-nine years. The brothers had no family to take over the business once they died, so a short-term contract was a no-fucking-brainer. The mill opened its doors, employing hundreds of people, making the plant the third largest company within a hundred miles of Bellingham. Business was booming, thanks to cheap and abundant local lumber, easy access to shipping and receiving goods, and of course, the cheap fucking power. But the brothers faced a financial setback: the unexpectedly high cost of waste removal."

"Waste removal?" I ask, twisting my head toward him.

"Yep. Industrial factories create super toxic byproducts that have to be hauled away to a waste management center, and it ain't cheap to remove, five or six times the cost of electricity. You ever hear about the Triangle of Death in Italy? Look it up sometime. So, being the greedy business bastards the brothers were, they cut a corner. Instead of paying for waste removal, they dumped the toxins into Bellingham Bay and the surrounding woods. Soon, their workers and others in town were getting sick, some died, lawsuits followed, and the Anderson Mill closed their doors, and to my knowledge, the brothers were never seen again."

"I hope those assholes got what they deserved, a slow, painful—"

"Stop the car!" Carter yells.

"What?"

"Stop!"

The brakes squeak as the Beast slows to a stop.

"Oh shit. Kill your headlights," Carter whispers urgently. "Look."

I follow the direction of his gaze. To the left of the steel-roofed building is a Whatcom County squad car parked beneath an overhang.

"What's *that* doing here?"

"I don't know,"

"Should we leave?"

"Hell no. We're not letting one pig sidetrack us from what we're after." Carter scans his head from side to side. "There! Take us toward those roll-up doors. Do you see 'em?"

I don't *want* to see them, but I do. They're on the right side of the building, lit with a flood light. I take a deep breath. "Carter, maybe we should just forget this whole toilet paper thing and—"

He fixes me with a stony gaze. "We're gonna

be fine. That sheriff's car could have been sitting there for who knows how long? Hell, it could be abandoned here for all we know. Let's get a move on. We're losing precious time, brother."

There's that word again.

7. Room for One More

The Beast moves slow and steady like a nocturnal predator, creeping toward the right side of the steel-roofed building. The building's exterior is beaten to hell, its roll-up doors sealed shut and locked with heavy chains. Faded graffiti sprayed across the metal siding reads: TOXIC BASTARDS! SEE YOU IN HELL! There's another tag next to it: KILL THE MILL! DIE ANDERSON BROTHERS DIE! DIE!

Yikes, tell me how you *really* feel.

I back my beauty to the loading dock, and through my rearview mirror, I see a sign that reads GNIPPIHS. It takes a beat to decipher the message: SHIPPING. I kill the engine and ask, "What's the plan?"

Rummaging through his backpack, Carter replies, "The plan is to stay close and protect ourselves at all costs and when we find the TP, we stuff your Beast with as much ass-paper as she can handle." He smiles, then pulls something out of his backpack. "Here," he says, "keep this on you."

He hands me a wood-handled flathead screwdriver. "Never leave home without it," he adds. He holds up a black flashlight and checks the battery's condition, turning it on and off, then stuffs the light back into his sack and leaps out of his seat. He sprints up the cement stairs leading to the landing dock, waving at me to hurry.

I catch up with Carter, who's now standing beside a metal man door and wheeling on its handle. He asks for the screwdriver. I hand him the tool, and with one quick jab, he jams the tip into the keyhole, then uses both hands and twists counterclockwise until there's a satisfying snap. Grinning, Carter returns the flathead, eyebrows raised. I pocket it and follow him inside.

The door swings shut behind us, and we're swallowed by darkness. I can't even see my hands. My senses are reduced to my ears and nose: our sodden shoes squeaking, and a suffocating stench like mothballs. I consider retreating and telling Carter that I'll be in the Beast, but when a beam of light from his flashlight illuminates the room and objects come into focus, my disquiet recedes.

Carter pans the light, revealing wooden workbenches and empty shelves webbed with spider silk. The beam exposes packing peanuts, tape rolls, hand carts, and in the far corner, cardboard boxes stacked in a pyramid.

"There!" Carter says, then takes off.

He's quick, and I'm slow, but I do my best to keep up with the guy. When Carter is close to the base of the pyramid, he shoves the butt end of the flashlight in his mouth and uses his free hands to wipe away a thick layer of dust from a box, exposing the letters APM TP.

Carter yanks the flashlight from his mouth, hands it to me, and says, "Aim it here."

The handle is sticky from saliva, but I ignore it. I shine the light against the box as he tears it open, then like Rafiki in *The Lion King* holding up baby Simba, Carter raises a shrink-wrapped four-pack of toilet paper above his head. "Jackpot. Grab as much as you can."

The boxes are light but large and unwieldy, and after the fifth or sixth trip to the Beast, my muscles show signs of fatigue. After the seventh or eighth, I hear a noise inside the warehouse.

"Carter," I whisper. "Did you hear that?"

"Hear what?" he asks, fumbling his flashlight.

"I hear someone. Footsteps, maybe."

Carter scans the darkness with his light, revealing nothing. "You're hearing things," he tells me, reaching for another box. But then I hear the sounds again, and this time, they're unarguably human footsteps approaching us.

CLOMP CLOMP!

Carter stiffens and presses his finger against his lips. "Quiet," he murmurs, then jerks his head, signaling for me to follow.

I tiptoe after him around the stacked boxes, and breaths held, we crouch with our backs against the cardboard. The footsteps become louder, clearer.

CLOMP CLOMP!

A light probes the warehouse, then a man's voice resounds, "This is the Whatcom County Sheriff's Department."

The hairs on my head stand on end, and the voice in my mind screams: *RUN! HIDE! SURRENDER!*

Carter shoves his palm over my lips. I can hear the deputy walking toward us.

"Show yourselves with your hands above your head and nobody gets hurt!"

Carter's hand drops from my face and unzips his backpack. He pulls out a bottle and a rag. He pops the top and pours a liquid onto the fabric. The odor is overwhelmingly tangy and sour, and instantly my eyes water.

A woman's voice crackles over the deputy's walkie-talkie. "Unit nine-two, what's your ten-twenty? Over."

"Unit nine-two here. I'm inside level one, returning to headquarters with cargo at 2300 hours. Over."

"Roger that, unit nine-two. Over and out."

Carter bolts upright from his squatting stance, and with his rag clenched in his fist, he maneuvers around the boxes and charges toward the deputy. He jumps on the deputy's back, knocks the flashlight out of his hand, and shoves the stinking rag over his face.

In the dim light, I watch their bodies twisting, falling on the cement floor. The deputy's boots kick out, grunting until he's not. Carter cackles triumphantly, "Come on out. It's safe."

I approach Carter. He's got his knee pressed on the deputy's back like a hunter claiming his trophy. I prod the deputy with the toe of my boot. He's unresponsive.

"Is he ... dead?" I ask. I feel feverish.

Carter shrugs then leans down, pressing two fingers against the deputy's throat. "Nope, but we better move fast before he wakes up."

The deputy's walkie-talkie crackles to life with a panicked voice calling for backup. Carter unclips the radio from the deputy's hip, twists the volume knob until it falls mute, then tosses it aside. "Let's finish what we started," he says as he brushes past me, returning to the toilet paper stash. I continue to stare at the motionless deputy.

He's young and skinny and looks vaguely familiar. Did we go to the same school? Whatever, just some rookie with a shitty work shift.

I'm shoving a box of TP into the driver's seat when Carter tells me, "There's room for one more." He runs back into the warehouse. There isn't any more room, so I have to make room. I use my knees to smash down the boxes and doing so, I get this stabbing pain. It's the screwdriver biting into my thigh. I pull it from my pocket and stash it underneath the driver's seat. Just then, I hear Carter yell, "He's waking up!"

I jump inside the Beast and start her up. Carter scurries into his shotgun seat and shouts, "Step on it!"

Adrenaline coursing through my veins, I break my rule about starting her cold. The Beast roars as it launches forward. Laughing like a madman, Carter yells, "Keep going! Haha! Keep going! We did it! Hahaha! We fuckin' got 'em!" We zip through the meadow, past the fence, up the embankment, and back on the road.

We did it. But what the fuck did we just do?

8. WORST-CASE SCENARIO

CARTER SUGGESTS WE REFRAIN FROM DRIVING on busy roads until we reach his Pops's place. I don't argue—I get it, I've watched enough heist flicks to understand it's best to keep a low profile after the fact. What twists my stomach in knots is what he says next: "Don't worry. There's a shortcut through the Falls."

Oak Falls—or simply known as the Falls among locals—is a small, secluded town in northeast Whatcom County. Its city limits encompass a mere three square miles, home to three hundred inhabitants. Around it are soaring mountains, rivers, even a horseshoe-shaped lake stocked with trout. It sounds like a delightful Hallmark card of a town, right? Well, it's not. The picturesque natural surroundings are nothing more than a sham. Oak Falls is home to the most crime per capita in the entire state.

When I was young, my mother prohibited me from going there, and believe me, I listened. The Falls is home to sketchy trailer trash, hillbilly crank addicts. Seriously, get this: There have been over thirteen *COPS* episodes that have taken place at Oak Falls. It seems as if the town makes local headlines every other week for something incredibly stupid. I've driven through the Falls once in my life, and only because the Beast would have run out of gas otherwise. To this day, I remember how fucked everything was. An entire town of dilapidated trailers and heaps of garbage everywhere. The Falls exudes an I-don't-give-a-fuck kind of neglect.

"We're four miles from the Falls," Carter says, adjusting the brightness of his phone's screen. Just hearing the fucking words *the Falls* causes my heart rate to spike.

It's getting late. My strength is fading and my hunger growing as adrenaline wears thin. I need a fix. I cook up a plan inside my head as I clench the wheel, doing thirty down a curvy back road: *I drive through this hellhole of a town and then I drop off Carter at Chuck's. We offload his share of the TP, then I head straight downtown to Brighter Days. I get zapped, then go home with minutes to spare before lockdown.*

I glimpse at the dusty cardboard boxes behind me through the rearview mirror, and seeing them packed to the Beast's ceiling triggers a crystal-clear image: the deputy sprawled out on the floor. Best-case scenario, he woke up with a hangover, groggy, and too embarrassed to tell anybody, so he forced himself to forget that the assault ever took place. Worst-case, he's pissed like a hornet and now we're wanted fugitives. I imagine the judge reading our crimes to a room full of jury:

Trespassing.

Theft.

Assault.

Attempted murder.

Guilty.

I have blood on my hands, and I'm as much to blame as Carter. I drove and destroyed property, stole, all premeditated.

Did the damn deputy get a good glimpse at Carter before he collapsed? There could have been cameras, witnesses, something that could connect us to him. The squad car—was there a recording device attached? My chest feels like it's going to cave in. *Breathe*, Max. Calm down, remember you're safe inside the Beast.

"Carter."

"Yeah." He keeps his face fixed to his phone.

"What was it that knocked the deputy out cold like that?"

"It's just a cocktail of household chemicals."

"Like ... what?"

He stops fiddling with his phone. "You know, cleaning stuff. Don't worry. He should be fine in a few days."

Should be fine?

Carter rolls down his window and shoves his head out. "Can you smell that?" he asks.

"What are you doing? You're letting all the cold air in the cab." I've had enough of Carter's shenanigans.

He ignores my question and asks again, "What do you smell?"

"I smell nothing except our freedoms stripped from us for the next ten-to-twenty years."

"Is that what this attitude is about?"

"Attitude?"

"Yeah, you're all stiff and you have that worried look on your face. Max, it's unhealthy to think like that."

"Like what?"

"Like obsessing over the worst-case scenario. Living in constant fear is horrible for your health."

"I'm not *afraid*. I'm realistic and logical."

"Well, stop it."

"Carter, you had me trespass, steal, and fuck man, you assaulted a deputy with some chemical shit. Tell me, how the fuck else should I act?"

"Max, all I'm saying is that it's not healthy to

worry so much. Shit man, I haven't seen you so wound up since that time we snatched those cases of sodas from your neighbor, remember?"

"Yeah, and I remember my neighbor finding out. And I remember my mother having a fit about it and being grounded for a fucking month." I slam my fist against the wheel. "That sucked!"

"Dude, your energy is at eleven. You gotta bring it down to a three for me, so how about this: Instead of *worrying* about the what-ifs of the past, embrace our little victory. I mean, look at all that paper behind us. We're set up for whatever doomsday scenario—"

"So you want me to just *chill out* and that will make it all better?"

"No, just stop freaking out and obsessing over nothing."

"We just committed multiple felonies. I will not apologize for worrying about it."

"Who said anything about apologizing? Max, do me a favor and put your sorries in a sock for me because I'm not asking for 'em. You should be ecstatic. You're alive. We're fine. We did what we had to do. You watched the videos, right? Riots in the streets. Buildings on fire, reckless drivers, looting. What we did, in comparison, is peanuts."

"A room full of jury members and a judge will still give a shit about the peanuts, Carter."

"So what. We stole some old toilet paper from

an abandoned mill and had to fight our way out to do it. Nobody died. Nobody got *seriously* injured. Honestly, I just hate seeing you stress so much."

"I wouldn't be so stressed if I had—"

"If you had a zap?" Carter's voice turns scornful, and I hate it. "I know what you're dreaming about, Max. Don't worry. Once you drop me off, you'll be able to make it back to your little clinic and get all the precious light you need. It's no wonder why I haven't seen you in months. You're spending all your life inside a damn light booth."

"Hey, screw you. It's my job."

"Okay well, do me a favor, will ya? Can you bring it down a notch and focus on *this* moment instead of the past for five fuckin' minutes?"

As much as I hate to admit it, he's not wrong. I should cool it. What's done is done. I could have said no, I'm not doing it, no way, no how, it's not gonna happen old friend. I could have done many things differently, but I stuck with him. Fuck.

"Fine. I'll chill. I'm relaxed."

"Great. Now do us both a solid, roll down your window and tell me what you smell."

I lower my window, take an exaggerated gulp of air, and hold it in my lungs for a moment. The air is crisp, sweet, like a Washington apple.

"Well?" Carter asks.

I let out the air. "It's not so bad."

"Well, keep breathing that not-so-bad clean

Cascadian air, and keep us due east. Oak Falls is—"

I interrupt him. "What the hell is this?" Straight ahead, the Beast's headlights shine upon a school bus parked sideways, stretching across both lanes.

Carter stiffens in his seat. "I don't know. Slow down and keep your eyes peeled."

I let off the gas, coasting until I park the Beast a car length from the roadblock. The bus has been painted black and appears unoccupied. Unease washes over me. Something about this scene feels off, like I've seen this before, and for the life of me I can't think where or when. "We gotta turn around!"

"Max, we're not turning around." Carter peers through his passenger window. "Do you think we can go around this hunk of tin?"

The Beast's headlights create a reflective halo glow against the bus, too weak to expose the surroundings.

"I'm not sure," I tell him.

Carter unbuckles his seat belt. "Let's see what the fuck is going on then."

We walk toward the edge of the road near the bus's rear, and Carter shines his flashlight down a rocky drop-off. "Your Beast is tough, but I don't think she can make it through this baloney. There has to be a way around the other side or—"

The wind picks up and I can't hear what he's saying. I lower my head and shield it with one arm against the brutal cold. Looking down at the wet asphalt, I see a growing shimmer. Headlights are approaching us.

"Carter, we have company."

He mutters under his breath, "Shit." Cracking his neck, he says, "Let me do the talking here."

A diesel Ford truck pulls up and parks beside the Beast. Its lights shine blindingly onto us. I hear the truck's doors creak and slam shut, and four silhouettes emerge to stand in a row in front of the Ford. The tallest among them says with a hillbilly drawl, "Look at dis horseshit."

Carter responds, "It's a little late for school, don't you think?"

"Yes sir-ee," the man says, now walking toward us.

Carter shines his flashlight on his face. It's a chalky, middle-aged guy with bright ginger mullet and a handlebar mustache of matching hue. He's wearing a trucker cap and an oil-stained t-shirt. Mr. Mullet stops. He looks back toward his three companions. "Would you look here, a goddamn school bus all cattywampus on the road."

He spits a thick, phlegm-filled loogie onto the street. "Ain't that a hoot? Well, you fellas are in some real good fortune. I got a ten-ton winch on my Ford that oughta move dis sonofagun just fine. Now, how 'bout lendin' me a hand?"

I glance at Carter, and he nods. "Sure thing, mister," he says.

We follow Mr. Mullet to his truck, and I take notice of the others standing in the shadows. They're kids—all three have the same bright ginger hair, the tallest of them with wispy orange hairs sprouting above his lip. Siblings? Cousins? I don't care. I just don't like the fact that we're outnumbered two to one, even if three of them are half our size.

Mr. Mullet walks to the rear bed of his truck and hollers, "See here, I got me this winch a while back. Best dang money I ever spent. You wouldn't believe the stuff I had 'er yank." He spits again. "This ten-ton powerhouse's hauled fallen trees, boulders, and can ya imagine, even a goddamn school bus a couple hours ago."

"What did you say?" Carter asks.

Mr. Mullet smiles crookedly, then I hear a hissing sound followed by an intense burning sensation all over my face. My eyes—they feel like they're going to explode in my skull. Carter screams, "Fucking mace!"

I drop and roll around on my back in agony, and the last thing I hear before blacking out is Mr. Mullet's voice. "Ain't personal. Just plain ol' business."

"Max! Max! Wake up!"

My eyelids feel as if they've been stapled shut. I pry them apart using my fingernails and I see two Carters. It takes a moment before they resolve into one. I try standing but my bones ache, so I sit on the wet pavement cross-legged, rubbing my skull and trying not to puke.

"They took it," Carter moans. "All of it. Robbed. Those fucking ginger crooks!"

"Took what?"

"All the toilet paper, man. Look!"

Carter's face is as blurry as an impressionist painting, but I can still make out the deep lines in his forehead as he shakes with anger. I struggle to my feet and lurch toward the Beast. He's right—the entire cab is empty. All the toilet paper is gone except one shrink-wrapped roll tucked underneath the driver's seat. I toss it to Carter.

"Here, they missed this."

He catches it, then squishes the roll as if it was a stress ball. "Fuck. I can't believe I let those hicks trick us like that. Fucking school bus blocking the fucking road. I should have seen that coming. All that work for—"

"Cops," I blurt out.

"What? No, we're not calling the police, Max. What the hell—?"

"No. I saw this before on an episode of *COPS*.

The crooks used a school bus to block the road and—"

"Fucking balls. So *this* was a goddamn re-run," Carter mumbles, tossing the toilet paper back inside the Beast. "We need to get this shit off our faces and get the hell out of here. You think you can drive?"

My head pounds, pulsating waves of nausea cutting through me. "I can hardly see." I yank the keys from my front pocket and toss them over. "You're driving us out of here."

I stumble toward the passenger seat as Carter fires up the engine. Even with a splitting headache, I hear her RPMs. "Warm her up," I remind him.

"Sure," Carter says, scratching at his face.

I squint to focus on the clock. "What time is it?"

"It's time to get off the road and get medical care."

"The closest emergency room is in Belling—"

"No hospitals. My cousin Sunshine, she's a naturopath."

"Sunshine?"

"Yeah. She's was a grade older and—"

"Of course I remember." She was only my biggest high school crush. "I thought she moved away?"

"She did and now she's back, and she's living

in Glacier. She can help us. Just sit tight and relax. You know, you took most of that spray to the face like a champ. I got hit with half of what you had."

"I did, didn't I? Take it all to the face?"

"I can't imagine what kind of hurt you're in. Brother, I'd still be on the ground rolling."

A second wave of pain washes over me. I squint, cross-eyed, and now I see three Carters sitting next to me. I set my seat horizontal and lean back. I hear the transmission turn, then the wheels roll. The engine rumbles soothingly beneath my seat.

As we chug along in miserable silence, my mind drifts to Sunshine. It's been years, and I doubt she even remembers me; I was just her cousin's quiet friend, his shadow. And tonight of all nights, I'm going to see her?

9. You owe me

I wince at the horrible crunching of rocks tearing into the Beast's undercarriage as Carter swerves onto a gravel road. "We're here," Carter says as he parks.

I can't see much beyond the sheets of low-hanging mist and light rain pitter-pattering on the glass, but *here* seems to be a double-wide beside a weather-worn barn, backed up to thick woods.

Carter kills the engine, tosses me my keys, then asks, "How are you feeling?"

I feel like someone put a garden rake to my face, seasoned my cuts with salt and lime, then cooked me over a fire pit. "I've been better."

"Right. So, what do you say we get you cleaned up?"

We exit the cab and Carter helps me up some wooden stairs leading to a porch, where a light shines above a storm door. He thumbs the doorbell and a chime echoes through the mobile home. A throbbing silent moment passes. As Carter reaches toward the button again, a voice calls out, "Who is it?"

"It's me!" Carter yells, leaning his face closer to the door.

"Cuz?" the voice asks, followed by footsteps. I hear the deadbolt fold into the door and the hinges squeak, then the porch light falls upon Sunshine's face. My stomach drops as I marvel at her standing behind the storm glass barrier. Her dark hair is pulled into a ponytail at the crown of her head, making her look like a genie out of a magic lamp. She glances at me for a millisecond, long enough to freeze-frame her mesmerizing pale blue eyes and rich almond skin.

"Carter?" she asks. "Is that ... Max? What happened to your face?" She recoils. "Do you have HIT? Are you sick?"

"No, we're fine," Carter says. "Well, Max isn't so hot. Some ginger thieves maced us."

"What? Get inside, quick," she says, swinging the storm door open. "Follow me to the kitchen."

Inside to the left, a loveseat faces a flatscreen. The tube is blurry but I can hear someone talking about the lockdown, reminding listeners that Phase Zero starts at six tonight. Shit. I've got to get to my clinic. I take a deep breath before catching up with the gang.

In the kitchen, Sunshine has her face plunged inside a refrigerator. I make my way to a barstool next to Carter, who's leaning against a countertop.

Sunshine pulls back from the fridge, holding a glass container. She pops the top off the jar and dunks a clean rag into the clear gel inside.

"Here, this will help." She passes me the rag. It stinks like sweet, earthy compost. "Go on, it's good for you," Sunshine urges me. "Put it on your face and keep it there. What about you, Carter, do you need one?"

"Don't worry about me. I didn't get sprayed as hard as Max."

The soaked rag is icy and soothing to the touch. I hear Sunshine rummaging through the cupboards as she asks, "Are you two hungry? I haven't eaten all day."

"I could eat," Carter says promptly.

"Max, how about you?"

I feel like a fool with my face covered in wet, stinking cloth, so I try to downplay my insatiable hunger. "Nah, I don't want to be a bother."

"No bother. Come on, eat something. Do you guys like red curry?"

"Hell yeah I do," Carter says.

"Well, sure, but only if it's not a problem," I tell her.

"No problem at all. Keep resting, make yourself at home, and let me know if you need anything. Keep that rag on your face until it feels better."

"Sounds good. Thanks Sunshine."

"Yeah, thanks cuz. I owe you one," Carter says.

"You owe me a *few*, mister," she replies, which must be some inside joke because they both burst into chuckles.

I hear Sunshine humming to herself as she pulls out ingredients for our meal. My ass is aching on the hard kitchen stool, so I excuse myself and make my way toward the loveseat in the adjacent room, lowering the rag just enough to navigate. There's a news anchor on the tube, split-screened with Dr. Howson discussing HIT. I sit and raise the cloth back over my closed eyes, focusing my hearing on the televised voices.

"Doctor Howson, there are viewers who believe that the Phase Zero lockdown is too strict. They're concerned that this new protocol will create more damage to an already struggling economy. Do you care to comment?"

"Well, as you know, I'm not an economist, so I can't comment on behalf of our economy. But as a medical professional, I strongly support Phase Zero. The isolation protocols implemented are key until we develop a cure. Sealing off our borders, grounding flights, and quarantine will be prudent in containing the spread of this outbreak."

"Do you have the latest death count, Doctor?"

"So far, we're at 3042 and counting, and even more in critical condition."

Death.

Six feet under.

You.

Me.

Everyone.

I feel dizzy. The rag feels suffocating all of a sudden, and I tear it off my face and open my eyes, breathing unevenly.

"Thank you, Doctor Howson. That's all the time we have for now, so remember, Washingtonians, be smart and stay safe inside your homes. Up next, we have the latest schedule of food supplies distribution. Stay tuned to find out when your delivery truck will arrive."

The news program cuts to a commercial. Sappy flute music gently plays as a drone shot soars toward a lush hillside with rows of what I believe are coffee plants. Dozens of farmers work the fields. Their straw hats block the sun as they smile to camera with blank black stares. The camera zooms in on a farmer's hands plucking coffee beans and placing them in a wicker basket.

The narration begins.

"Our famous Seattle coffee begins with the

world's finest beans. We maintain an eco-friendly approach by handpicking each beautiful bean before it makes its way to you."

The scene dissolves to a cozy coffee shop with upper-middle-class suburban mothers sipping on white cups, smiling, exposing their bleached teeth. The scene resembles one of those overly cheerful pharmaceutical commercials with exaggerated acting.

"Remember, to serve the community, our Washington State drive-throughs will remain open through Ph—"

I find the remote and kill the tube, then slap the rag back on my face and drift in and out of sleep for a while, I'm not sure how long. Eventually, my skin feels a lot better, and so does the rest of me.

Discarding the rag, I pull myself up and move toward a picture hanging in the room. It's a dusty framed portrait of Sunshine and her parents that looks like it was taken at a Sears studio many years ago. Sunshine sits cross-legged between her folks, her face full of braces. She has her mother's hair and her father's skin and eyes. They seem genuinely content together and—

"Yo, Max!"

Carter appears holding a pair of glass bottles.

"I got a cold brewski for you if you like," he says, raising the beverages to eye level. He hands me one and we clink glass. "Food is ready out back," he tells me.

I take a sip then follow Carter through the kitchen, which is fragrant from Sunshine's recent cooking. A screen door leads us outside to a grassy path that wraps around the house and toward the barn. We enter the barn through a wooden Z-bar door. Carter guides me past a perforated plastic wall, then—BAM! I'm hit with a blast of electric blue light.

My eyes adjust. Blue bulbs hang from the barn's rafters, beaming down on a jungle of prehistoric-looking potted plants. The plants are huge, each the size of a VW Bug. The room is pungent, humid, and hot as hell, and I begin sweating bullets. It must be over a hundred degrees in here. Carter sticks his face in front of a rotating fan, sidestepping to keep up with the head as it swivels.

I hear Sunshine's voice from across the barn. "Guys, I'm back here."

We shove off toward her call, through a door that opens up to what looks like a makeshift lab cluttered with scientific instruments—glass beakers overflowing with liquids and powders, sputtering Bunsen burners, microscopes, digital scales, and stuff I don't even recognize.

Sunshine rests on a bohemian-brown recliner. Beside her are two chairs butted against a coffee table that holds up a serving bowl of steaming rice noodles topped with red curry.

"Come, sit, eat," she invites us.

Carter and I pile our plates high with the red-sauced noodles and take our seats, thanking her. We chow down, guzzle our beers, and Carter belches the ABCs. The cousins burst into laughter as if it were another inside joke, and I feel like the third wheel, which reminds me of high school and how I was never in on anyone's joke. I've always felt on the outside, never in, as if I don't exist. I take a gulp of liquid courage, then another, trying to build up enough bravery to speak up, but the question I finally muster sputters out as an incoherent sentence. "Sunshine. Work. Is. You?"

She looks at me, head tilted and obviously confused, but Carter saves my ass. Without missing a beat he adds, "I think what Max is trying to ask is: What have you been up to?"

Sunshine flashes a smile and replies, "Oh, well, I've been busy as a bee. Working all the time."

"Are those giant plants you got in the back room your *work*?" Carter asks, then stuffs another forkful of noodles down his throat.

"As a matter of fact, yes. Those are a special variety of aloe vera, and I've been experimenting, extracting their essence and converting it into a gel that will heal damaged human cells."

"So it's some kind of medicine? The same stuff that you put on my face?" I ask.

Sunshine nods with a mouthful of beer.

"Where did you learn a thing like that, cuz?" Carter asks.

Sunshine swallows and replies, "I haven't told you?"

Carter shakes his head.

"Well, I heard a rumor about a small village in Thailand where the average lifespan is ninety-two years. I looked into it and it's true. I wanted to understand why, so I went there and discovered that the locals use a native variety of aloe vera to boost their immune systems. Western medicine already knows that aloe helps with burns, cuts, and bruises. But this variant is special, stronger. So for three years, I was lucky enough to intern with the village healer and learn how to grow it and work with it."

"And it's safe?" I ask her.

"You tell me, Max. How does your face feel?"

I'd almost forgotten that I'd been maced. I drag my fingertips against my cheek—it's smooth to the touch. "I feel brand new."

"Here. Try this too." Sunshine tosses me a dropper vial of liquid. I turn it in my hands and see that she's slapped a yellow smiley face sticker on it. "It's the same stuff but concentrated. Just squeeze a few drops on your tongue."

I unscrew the top and aim the tip of the dropper into my mouth. I squeeze the rubber end, and liquid pools on my tongue. The concentrate tastes sweet like lime Kool-Aid and tingles in the back of my throat. I feel subtly refreshed.

"Woah, easy there," Sunshine says. "Next time, just keep it to a few drops. You can have that vial. I have plenty."

I tilt my head to the side. "Are you sure?"

She winks, then twists toward Carter. "Now tell me, why would someone unload a can of mace on you guys in the first place?"

Carter swallows a mouthful of beer. "Well, if your parents were still around, they might have gotten a kick out of this."

"Oh?"

"Yeah, because Max and I broke into the Anderson Mill."

Sunshine drops her beer. Glass shatters all over the floor. "You did what?"

"We broke inside the mill," Carter repeats.

"How? Why?" she asks, ignoring the spilled beer foaming on the floor.

"We broke through the fence with Max's Suburban. Remember her, the Beast? We were, you know, stockpiling essential supplies, but on our way back there was this roadblock, and then this truck with ginger assholes showed up. They sprayed us and took all the ass-paper that we grabbed from the mill."

She falls into the cushion of her chair, chuckling. "Jesus. You're right. My parents would have gotten a kick out of it if they were still here."

"Where did your parents go?" I ask.

She catches her breath and tells me they didn't go anywhere, they died of mercury poisoning, then bursts into hysterical laughter. I look at Carter and he shrugs.

"Sorry," Sunshine says, wiping tears from her face. "My parents' death isn't funny. It's just that I've been trying to get inside that goddamn mill for a year. I've needed samples, you know, evidence linking the Andersons to the mercury that killed my parents. And after countless months of bullshit—I even got arrested once for trespassing—all I had to do was get in touch with you guys?" She exhales as if letting out a breath full of bong smoke. "But, you're telling me some redheads stole the paper that you stole from the mill?" She swipes Carter's beer from his hand and takes a gulp. "Fucking classic."

"Yeah, but cuz, we still have one roll. You want it?"

"Of course I do, but what about you guys?"

"All yours," I say. "Let's call it payment for your services."

Sunshine protests, but Carter says he'll be

right back then takes off, leaving her and me alone. Shit. I don't know what to say, so I act like I'm thinking by rubbing my jaw until she leans toward me.

"Max. How long has it been since we've seen each other?"

She pulls her ponytail from her face and adjusts her position, sitting with her legs folded like a pretzel. I get this knot twisted inside my guts because I know precisely when we saw each other: last day of school, my sophomore year. Sunshine was leaving the school's parking lot in her Volkswagen Jetta. She waved at me—at least I hope she intended the wave for me—and as I reciprocated the gesture, I tripped on a crack in the sidewalk and fell face first to the curb.

"Jeez, I don't know?" I mumble. "It must have been high school, right?"

She nods. "I think so."

Silence descends and I wish there were music playing, or a dog barking, or a fucking earthquake, anything that would distract the fact that I'm blowing it right now. Then Sunshine smiles and kills the awkward silence by asking another question. "What have you been up to since?"

"Well ... I have a business. *Had*, I guess. Brighter Days. Umm, that's the name. It's a light therapy clinic where people use medical light booths to help with anxiety."

Her mouth gapes and she shakes her head. "Max, that's exciting."

It's nothing, I'm the business's most popular customer—

"Tell me, what lights are you using at your clinic?"

"I have six light booths, each with four 10,000 LUX LEDs. They're much smaller than the ones you have beaming down on your aloes, and yours are so much warmer than mine. What are you working with?"

"I have a ray of 40Ks that I keep between 440 and 520 nanometers, which encourages chlorophyll absorption, photosynthesis, and rapid growth for my plants. So yeah, my lights get hot. I wouldn't recommend them for human use, but hey—" Sunshine leans in closer. "Maybe you could help me. I'm having trouble with this light timer and could use a—"

"Here, it's all yours," Carter says, barreling into the room. He tosses the toilet paper roll to Sunshine. She catches it and holds it up to her face.

I haven't seen the toilet paper in bright light, and now that I'm looking at it in her well-lit lab, I can see that it's a nasty cream-of-corn shade. I would never in a million years use this stuff on my ass, especially if the paper contains traces of mercury. Fucking Carter.

Sunshine examines the roll. "I can't believe it ... amazing ... I've gotta analyze the chemical content right away. Holy crap guys, thank you. I'll be up all night testing this." She gets up eagerly.

It dawns on me—Phase Zero. I ask if anyone has the time. Sunshine peers at her wristwatch and tells me it's half past five. Suddenly, memories of the events from earlier today come crashing down on me all at once. The marauding punks. The car wrecks. The gunshots. Hurtling through the fence. Trespassing and theft. The deputy, face down. The gingers. The mace. The memories wrap around me like a python, squeezing the life out of me. I'm about to have a panic attack. I need a fucking fix *right fucking now*.

"I have to go," I tell them as I stand.

"Where are you going?" Carter asks, narrowing his eyes.

"I'm not kicking you guys out. You're welcome to stay, I have plenty of room," Sunshine says.

"Thanks, but I have to go downtown. I need my booths."

"You want to go back to that war zone we narrowly escaped? I don't think—"

"No—You don't understand. I need my lights. Without 'em, I—"

"What about the lights here? Won't they do the trick?"

"It's not a trick, Carter. Besides, they're not the same thing."

Carter shrugs. He's got that look of disappointment on his face again.

Sunshine says, "If you need more aloe, Max, you know where to find me."

"Thanks." I extend my hand clumsily toward her for a shake, but she swats it away and gives me a proper hug. She smells wonderful, like lemongrass and cinnamon. "Bye Max," she says, then walks toward her lab equipment, tossing the TP roll from hand to hand.

For a moment, I'm torn by conflicting emotions as I watch her fiddle with her gear. Could I leave in the morning? No. There's no way I'll make it through the night without a serious meltdown.

10. Did I fucking stutter?

Outside, it's pouring buckets. I fire up the V8 and watch the RPM needle settle a tick above 1500. I should wait and let her warm up, but I hammer on the gas and steer her westbound on a deserted road toward the I-5 South on-ramp. I have her wiper blades moving at full speed but I still can't see much, so I pop on the high beams. Like my Beast, I'm moving on all cylinders, running on high-octane anxiety, obsessing over one thing and one thing only: getting a fix.

I slow down a quarter mile before my exit and roll down my window for a whiff of fresh air, but it stinks of gunpowder and sulfur, and my eardrums ring from the sounds of sirens and screams. It's too much, so I roll it back up as I exit the Interstate.

I stop at a light, and for a moment, downtown

is quiet. *Creepy* quiet. The crosswalk signal counts down: four, three, two, one. The light turns green. I shove forward, and as I'm halfway through the intersection, a tow truck barrels past the Beast. Shit! I pump the brakes and skid to a stop.

The reckless tow truck driver continues down Railroad Avenue. I notice that the truck is pulling the remains of the Firebird and BMW wreckage from earlier. Those poor bastards. Took them long enough. I glance at Beast's clock: six minutes to six.

Downtown is Armageddon, Judgment Day, fucking end-of-the-world shit. Main Street resembles the aftermath of a war with smashed storefronts, overturned trash cans, and what looks like empty tear gas canisters and the shattered remains of a Molotov cocktail smoldering on the ground.

My heart rate spikes and I take a deep breath. I should pull over and chill out but there's no time for a break. I mentally reiterate my simple plan: Get zapped, go straight home. Don't get caught.

I'm close, just one block away with butterflies flapping wildly in my gut. I can almost *feel* my soothing lights warming my skin as I make the last left on Bay Street. I park the Beast and run toward my clinic. My short-lived excitement is replaced by frustrated rage when I see a metal chain across my front door. *What the fuck.*

I run up and take a closer look. Some asshole

has bolted my entrance shut. I sprint around the corner to the lobby window to look inside, but it's boarded up with a thin sheet of plywood. A black Sharpie scribble across the wood reads: CLOSED BY ORDER OF PHASE ZERO.

I pound the board until my knuckles bleed, then I switch to kicks. My foot smashes through the timber, stopping short of the glass. I squint through the hole I've created. I can see that my chairs are tossed to the side, my check-in desk destroyed, and my booths—all but one is missing. I wrench at the plywood trying to widen the opening. I've got to get in there, one way or another.

As I'm tugging on the board, I hear a voice from behind. "Sheriff's department! Turn around with your hands above your head."

Fuck. I raise my palms to the sky then turn. A deputy limps toward me. As he gets closer, I see that his skin is discolored as if from a nasty rash.

"It's past six," he barks. "What the hell are you doing outside your residence?"

The Beast's clock must be slow. Nobody's perfect.

"Hey! Can you hear me, shithead?" he yells.

I straighten my posture. "Yes, sir. I can hear you. I was on my way home, sir." My father always advised me to address any authority figure as *sir*.

"Oh, were you?" He turns his gaze to the

busted plywood. "Looks like you're trying to break into this establishment."

"This is my business, sir."

"Oh is it? Well, what does that sign say?"

"It says closed, sir."

"That's correct. Now, it looks to me like you don't *have* a business." What an asshole. He scratches his neck, coughs, then tells me to keep my hands up and turn back around to face the building. I do as he says with no quick movements. Slow and steady.

"Is that your black Chevy parked at the curb?"

"Yes, sir."

"You haven't been up north tonight, have you?" he asks. He shoves me against the plywood and cuffs me.

"North, sir?" I ask with my cheek pressed up against wood.

"Did I fucking stutter? Have you been up north today? At the old Anderson Mill?"

"No. No, sir." Shit. Is this the guy from the mill?

I hear loud static, followed by a female voice shrieking from the deputy's radio. "Calling all units. We have a ten-forty-five in progress. I repeat, calling all units."

The deputy sighs. "You're coming with me, shithead."

Deputy Asshole tosses me into the back of his

squad car. I peer out and see him snapping a photo of the Beast's license plate. He slides into the front, hits the siren, then flips a bitch, and I watch my clinic and Beast fade away into the distance. My heart sinks.

11. Short of a Meat Wagon

Deputy Asshole hurls us through town. He's reckless, intentionally taking corners going way too fast and laughing as I bounce back and forth on the hard plastic seats like a fucking pinball. The metal cuffs dig into my wrists. After a while I wonder if I'm still in Whatcom County.

Eventually the squad car drives onto an unmarked driveway leading to a stone building encircled by a barbed-wire fence. Deputy Asshole continues, passing a guard with an assault rifle slung over his shoulder and a 9mm on his hip. The guard looks familiar ... Donut shop Larry? He stands proudly at a gate with a sign that reads CHECKPOINT. They nod to each other and the deputy continues toward the back of the building, where a handful of parked squad vehicles are in a lazy line.

Deputy Asshole drags me by my cuffs toward a door and pushes me through head first. Inside, I'm greeted by a banner that says: PHASE ZERO UNIT ONE - SHERIFF'S DEPARTMENT.

I take in the scene inside the precinct. Some deputies are shuffling papers, and others are on the phone. A group seems to be reenacting the day's arrests to each other, chortling as they describe the skulls they've cracked. The room stinks like dirty feet and burned coffee. Deputy Asshole escorts me down a hall to an empty jail cell the size of a broom closet and pushes me inside.

From behind me Deputy Asshole says, "You don't have any weapons on you, do you, shithead?"

"Weapons? No, sir."

"We'll see about that." He frisks me and seizes my wallet, keys, phone, and the vial of aloe concentrate from Sunshine. He flips me around like a rag doll and shoves the vial into my face. "What the fuck is this?"

"I don't know, sir."

"Right, we'll see about that." He releases the cuffs from my wrist then locks the door behind me and stalks off.

I look around at my dismal surroundings. The tiny cell is cold, gray, and stinks like shit. There's a stainless-steel crapper in the corner about an inch from a twin-sized mattress on a steel frame soldered to the floor. I take a deep breath and try to settle into my new digs.

Across from me is a holding cell packed with inmates. One of them has his face shoved between two bars, and he's looking at me looking at him. He's dressed in black and has a medical wrap over his foot.

"Hey!" he yells with his head cocked to the side. "You're that bitch-ass with the black Suburban. You ran over my goddamn foot!"

Fuck, it's one of the gutter punks.

Ignoring him, I turn and curl up into a fetal position on the stiff bed. He screams, "Don't you turn your back on me you stupid fuck! Oh man, I can't wait until we're roommates. You're fucking dead!"

A deputy shouts, "Hey, bonehead! I thought I told you to shut the hell up."

I'm trying my damndest to steady my breath but it's no good, my mind runs wild. How long are they going to keep me here? What will they do to me? Am I going to need a lawyer? What about my one phone call? My heart rate spikes as I toss and turn. *Breathe*, I remind myself. But the world starts spinning. The deputies' voices outside the cell coalesce into a muddled ball of horror, their words penetrating into my brain. *Roadblocks. Tear gas. Supply chain. Quarantine. Riots.* They're laughing and hollering and it's giving me a jackhammer headache. I fold my elbow over my face and imagine a peaceful place: driving the Beast, heading straight into a magnificent sunset—

BAM!

I look over and it's Deputy Asshole with a billy club, clobbering the iron bars of my cell. He's accompanied by a tall white guy dressed in a black suit. The new guy is closed-lipped and brown-eyed, with a full head of dark hair slicked back and glistening as if he's dumped an entire can of styling mousse on his head.

Deputy Asshole says to Mr. Mousse, "Make it quick," then leaves.

Make *what* quick?

Mr. Mousse tells me to come closer. His voice is a higher pitch than I would have guessed. He removes my driver's license from his pocket and begins to read the details of my identity out loud.

"Maxwell Maddison. Male. Five foot nine, one hundred fifty-five pounds, dark blond hair, hazel eyes, twenty-two years old, 5751 North Queen Street, Bellingham, Washington." His stare lifts from my ID to me as he sneers the final line, "Organ donor."

Mr. Mousse then stuffs my license into his suit. "Maxwell, do you know why you're here?"

"I was caught outside illegally during Phase Zero."

"Yes, but that's not *why* you're here, Maxwell.

You're here because, like ninety-nine percent of the state, you're categorized as less than human, disposable ... hell, you're nonessential, and as of right now, your human rights are nonexistent. You'll have no trial, no lawyer, and these men behind me are going to lock you up and do whatever the fuck they want to you. But you're in luck. I'm here to set you free."

My head tilts. "You are?"

Mr. Mousse smiles like I've asked him to say cheese for the camera. "You have two options. Option one, you can continue to be less than zero and rot behind bars. Or option two, you can become somebody useful by working for me."

"Let me get this straight, you can get me out of here if I work for you?" I ask skeptically.

"Of course. That's why I'm here. To give you a choice. Freedom."

"Why me? Why not any of those guys across the hall?"

"For starters, you don't have a record yet, but once they fingerprint you and stuff you into their system, I can't hire you. It would be illegal."

"What else?"

"Well, you appear to be in excellent physical health. Hell, let's throw in a third reason, and one might call it slight nepotism. Your *family* brought us together."

"My family?"

"Well yes. I know your mother. Anne."

"Really?"

"Yes, really. Your mother and I have only recently become acquainted."

How the fuck would he have met my mother? "So, what kind of work would I be doing for you, hard labor in a refinery until my back gives out?"

"No, not at all Maxwell. This isn't North Korea. I won't work you to death, quite the opposite. What I'm offering is a work-release program. You would move corpses for my business, J & J Funeral."

Dead bodies? I take a step back. "What kind of job is that?" I ask, trembling.

"It's an *essential* job and your only ticket out of here."

I back up until I hit the edge of my bunk and sit. Is this a joke?

"This job sounds like it frightens you. Don't fear, Maxwell. This isn't a suicide mission. You'll have all the proper safety gear when handling the deceased."

"For how long?"

"Until Phase Zero is over."

"Then I'm free to go?"

"Yes, but there is a catch."

Of course. Okay, I'll bite. "What's the catch?"

He pulls out my car keys from his suit jacket.

"This is a joint deal. I'll need you plus your Suburban."

"What? Why?"

"To move the bodies, of course. All my vans are working around the clock, so I'm short of a meat wagon. The deal is you *and* your Suburban will work for me. Now I don't have all day, Maxwell, so do we have a deal?"

"One question."

"Yes, go on."

"Do I get to go home when I'm not working?"

"No. This work release agreement will prevent you from going home."

"Where do I sleep then? Or shower or eat?"

"I have a private room for you at my headquarters with all the amenities and a fully stocked fridge. It's not fancy, but it's much nicer than the cement box you're in at the moment."

"Do I get to make phone calls, at least? My mother, she's—"

"Yes, I know all about your mother, Maxwell. I know she's at King County Care, and I assure you she's in excellent hands. I know the director over there personally. But to answer your question: No. You won't be able to contact the outside world. Your phone, your keys, everything will be in my custody until Phase Zero is lifted."

As I weigh my options, I glimpse the gutter punk across the hall. Our eyes meet. He slides his thumb across his throat suggestively, grinning, pantomiming the fate in store for me. Fuck this place. I'm a dead man if I stay here. "Okay, I'm in."

"Fan-fuckin'-tastic."

"When do I start?"

"Tomorrow morning, bright and early. My associate will collect you then. It's been nice talking with you, Maxwell. You just made a very wise decision."

Mr. Mousse spins on his heel and walks away down the hall, deputies nodding at him as he passes. I press my face between the iron bars and call out, "Hey mister, wait. What's your name?"

Mr. Mousse stops, flashes a bleached smile over his shoulder, and says, "The name's Jim, but *you'll* call me Boss."

12. YOUR HEAD WILL SPIN

IT'S IMPOSSIBLE TO CATCH ANY MUCH-NEEDED shut-eye inside my cell. For starters, there's a bright tangerine light above my bed beaming on my face, there's no pillow, and my blanket is ratty and stinks like used gym shorts.

But my real frustration is the deputies—they won't shut the fuck up. Like Sunday-game-day drunks, those half-wits spew continuous banter from their mouths. Loud, slurring, and squawking like roosters, they try to one-up each other's stories, arguing over who's taken down the most protesters and quarantine violators.

So instead of sleeping, I toss and turn on my rock-hard mattress. I'm exhausted, seeing double. I have four hands, twenty fingers, and four feet. Did I hallucinate Jim?

WHACK!

I sit up at what sounds like a slab of meat thumping against my cell bars. Standing in front of me is a large-framed man stuffed into a tan sheriff's uniform, pounding against the iron bars with his sausage-like fists. He has an ebony five-gallon cowboy hat covering his dome and a golden star over his left boob that reads SHERIFF EVANS.

Evans stops and laughs without a punchline, his double chins jiggling. He catches his breath then leans his tubby face toward me until his pimpled nose is just shy of the iron bars.

He's got a face I'd hate to see in a dark back alley, with sunken purplish eye sockets cradling stone-cold soulless eyes. Ancient acne scars crater his pasty skin. He's a goddamn gorilla with a gut that suggests he's been at the top of the food chain for too long.

He stares at me as I sit cross-legged on my bunk and after a moment, which feels like fucking forever, he barks in a baritone, nasally and wet. "Stand up, stupid. Put your hands behind your back and face the wall."

I jump to my feet, turn, and press my fingers against my lower spine. I hear the cell door squeak open, followed by Evans's heavy footsteps. I can feel the weight of his shadow looming over me. He exhales a warm breath that reeks of Old Spice and ketchup then grabs my wrists, and in one quick move, he has me cuffed.

Evans orders me to turn around and face him. I realize he's a full head and shoulders taller than me. "If you fuck around," he says, "I'll shove my size sixteen boot up your ass so fast your head will spin. Got it?"

"Yes sir. Sheriff sir."

"Don't get smart with me," Evans says as he thumps his colossal pointer finger against my sternum. "Jim must have thought you were *special*, getting you out of here. But you listen to me real good, boy, you're not special, you're just a lucky worm, a nobody, and when you fuck up, I'll be waiting. Now move it!"

Evans drags me by my elbow down the precinct hall past the bumbling deputies, shoves me into the back seat of a squad car, then slams the door. The car's suspension bottoms out when Evans crawls into the driver's seat. He fires up the engine and jams on the gas, knocking me backward.

Evans cruises through the early morning mist with his cherries-and-berries flashing, siren thankfully off. We pass the outskirts of downtown Bellingham. It's a ghost town. There's no one in sight among the boarded-up businesses already tagged with anti-Phase-Zero graffiti.

Miles later, the squad car turns onto a paved driveway leading to a gold-painted gate stamped with the letters J & J centered in cursive. Evans pulls up just before the gate alongside a marble tombstone with a chiseled epitaph:

J & J FUNERAL SERVICES

Embedded into the tombstone is a silver panel with a keypad. Evans rolls down his window and presses three buttons. There's a beep. Gears twist and the gate opens. Evans drives through, keeps left at a roundabout, and out my window appears a gothic building of cold gray stone and brick that looks preserved from a faraway time.

The morning sun glimmers upon the mortuary's narrow windows, revealing intricate stained glass. From its high roofs, spires reach toward the purple sky. The main entrance lies beneath a large pointed arch, and as we pass it, I can't help but feel a sudden rush of déjà vu. This place looks a lot like ...

Father's funeral.

I start sweating and hyperventilating as the memories of that day flood my thoughts. I can see his ghostly pale face cushioned against his casket's plush interior. His skin looks so cold and I feel so alone. I'm going to die and end up rotting in a wooden box *six feet underground and there's nothing I can do about it—NOTHING THAT I CAN DO ABOUT IT—*

"Relax kid, this ain't *your* funeral."

I snap out of it to see Evans eyeballing me through the rearview mirror.

He parks in a lot that butts up to the back side of the funeral home, next to a colossal metal warehouse with an industrial roll-up door. Evans keeps the engine idled as he pulls his ass out of his seat, yanks me from mine, and hauls me by the scruff of my neck toward a man door next to the roll-up.

He pounds his meaty fists three times above the doorknob, and within seconds, the door swings open. A guy wearing a silver hazmat suit pops into view, the hood thrown back to expose his long blond hair parted down the middle, cobalt-blue eyes, and a smile that shows off his oversized white teeth. He reminds me of a young Tom Petty.

"Hey Sheriff," the kid says with glee. "You brought us a new one, did ya?"

"Yep. Well, you know the drill, Noah. Call if you need anything."

"Yes Sheriff, you know I will," Noah replies, with an overly optimistic *Leave It To Beaver* inflection.

Evans releases a key ring attached to his utility belt and unlocks my cuffs. I watch my pallid fingers regain vibrancy as blood pours back into them.

"He's all yours," Evans says. "Oh, and tell Jim that he owes me one."

"Will do, Sheriff."

Evans leans into my ear and whispers, "Remember what I told you. No bullshitting around or you'll have a date with my size sixteen. You hear?"

I nod meekly and Evans waddles off. Noah beckons me inside then shuts the door. It's dim, with an intense smell that reminds me of dill pickles. Noah faces me, smiling for a second too long. "Come on," he says. "We have some preliminary work to do."

I try my best to keep up as he speed-walks through a labyrinth of shelves. I'm mildly impressed by how nimble he manages to be while rocking a hazmat suit.

"This warehouse," Noah says as he walks, "is 20,000 square feet, filled with everything we would ever need to move dead weight, including our meat wagons. This is our home base. We always leave from the warehouse at the start of our shift and return to the warehouse at the end. Now, before we dive any deeper, I need to take care of some onboarding procedures."

The maze opens up to a metal shipping container. Noah pulls open its door, and I follow him inside. A single bare bulb hangs from the ceiling, shining starkly upon a barber's chair. Noah says, "Sit, please," pointing at the chair. I take a seat on the black vinyl cushion. "Don't get too comfortable," he says cheerfully.

His demeanor morphs suddenly from a smiling, happy-go-lucky Tom Petty to a sharp-eyed and smirking David Bowie from *Labyrinth*. He mutters, "Go time," and even his voice has changed to a deeper, malevolent timbre. Two metal rings pop out from the armrests of the chair and lock around my forearms, pinning me down.

"What the hell is this?" I sputter, trying to slip away. Noah ignores my question. He itches the back of his neck like a flea-bitten dog then says, "This is going to sting a little."

"*What—*"

A sharp pain sends shocks through my body and I scream involuntarily. I look down, and there's a needle as thick as a chopstick piercing my left bicep. He has the butt end attached to a tube, connected to a bag with my name on it: M. MADDISON. I watch my blood ooze toward my name.

"What is this? What are you do—"

Noah's gloved fingers clamp down on my lips, silencing me. Before I can react, he seizes the fingers of my right hand and forces them onto a black ink pad. He then coerces my fingers onto a blank piece of paper, stamping my prints permanently onto the sheet.

"You're going to be recorded now," he says, shoving a handheld camera into my face. He clears his throat. "As of this moment, you are on work release. If you resist work, miss work, or are unfit for work, an officer will remove you to a designated detention center. If you understand what I'm telling you, and you comply with these consequences, say so by first stating your full name to the camera, then stating your consent." He releases my lips.

My muscles tighten up and I can't stop blinking, still in shock. A moment passes. I see the amber recording light on the camera and Noah's face next to it. He nods, motioning for me to speak. He mouths: *Say your name.* I swallow a lump, look into the lens, and tell him what he wants to hear.

Noah shuts off the camera and yanks out the needle, slapping a butterfly bandage over the wound. The metal rings retract, freeing me. He smiles, transformed back to a young and sweet Tom Petty.

"Welcome to the J & J team. Let's get you to your room."

I follow Noah as he exits the shipping container and moves toward a steel door at the far end of the warehouse. He flings it open, and we walk through into an ostentatious hallway with ornate trim and oil portraits hung on the walls.

"Come on, this way," Noah says. We pass one unmarked door after another. Our footsteps creak on the herringbone-patterned wood floors. Noah stops and tells me, "This is you," gesturing at a plain door.

Inside is a simple room with a bed and two more doors. Noah says, "The door on the left is a bathroom and the other is a closet with your work uniform, just like mine." He points at his hazmat suit. He then gestures toward a circular alarm bell hung above the entrance. "You can rest here until that alarm goes off. When you hear it, you get dressed in your suit as fast as you can and I'll come fetch you. Got it?"

He's gone before I can even answer, the door thudding shut behind him. I kill the lights and make my way toward the bed. It's surprisingly comfortable. Covering myself with a soft fleece blanket, I lay my head on a pillow and close my eyes. As I lie there, my mind races like a flipbook replaying scattered images of recent dreadful events. I toss and turn until I'm too exhausted to move, too tired to do anything but sleep.

13. You'll be fine

I awaken to the sound of a hammer beating steel. Construction? Marching band? No, it's the alarm above my door and the fucker won't stop. I press my fingers against my throbbing skull. My stomach aches and I burp up saliva that tastes acidic. I'm going to hurl.

I feel my innards pulsing as I rush toward the porcelain throne. On my knees with my head over the bowl, I watch red chunks explode from my mouth and into the toilet like Linda Blair's in *The Exorcist* until there's nothing left inside me. I force myself up and shove my head under the sink's faucet, wash my mouth, spit, then take a deep breath. I pluck the remaining crap from between my teeth, and once I'm clean, I stare into the basin. *Headache, vomiting blood.* Do I have HIT?

I shake the thought after I spot an unchewed

noodle floating in the bowl, remnants of dinner from the night before with Carter and Sunshine. Not blood, just red curry. I wonder what the cousins are up to now.

Thankfully, the alarm has stopped. I stumble out of the bathroom and move toward the closet. Inside, a silver hazmat suit hangs from a dowel. With reluctance, I hold it against my chest. The material is thick synthetic material with a fresh-from-the-factory scent. Clean ... Okay ... Great. I can do this. I unzip its front and climb into the protective tuxedo one leg at a time, finishing with a zipper that cuts underneath my chin and seals me from the outside air.

Within seconds, I hate the damn thing. The inner lining is sticky like a used condom. I unzip the hood, push it back to let fresh air in, and remind myself that it's this fucking job or getting shanked in jail.

Noah bolts into my room in his matching hazmat suit, his hood also thrown back. "How does it fit?" he asks.

"It fits," I reply, adjusting the plastic around my knees.

"Here, let me have a look." Like a jump cut in a film, one second he's standing at the door, then the next he's running his fingers over my suit's seams, telling me, "Our suits are custom. They have these built-in ventilators and high-grade biomaterial and lucky for you, yours is a perfect fit. Come on, we have a body to move."

We leave my room. The morning light pierces through stained glass windows, flooding the hallway with multicolored mosaic patterns. Despite being brighter, the vibe's the same—creepy as hell. In fact, the daylight adds haunting details to the sixteenth-century-style portraits hung on the walls, you know, the kind with those creepy peepers that follow you. As I follow Noah down the hallway, I catch my reflection in a brass-rimmed mirror and think, *This is a fucked-up movie titled* Max Maddison's Life. But it's not some Blockbuster. This shit is real.

Pinch me. This can't be happening. Yesterday, I was the proprietor of my own clinic and a free man. Fast forward some twenty-four hours and I've been attacked, maced, jailed, robbed of my Beast and my business, and now I have to move corpses during a fucking epidemic.

Noah stops in front of a door labeled WAREHOUSE. There's a numeric keypad beside the doorknob. He leans over it, blocking my view, and presses three buttons, answered by a beep and the satisfying sound of a lock unlatching. He swings the door open and walks through, me at his side.

We're back in the giant warehouse, now brightly lit by fluorescent shop lights above. As in the hallway, the increased light lets me observe previously unseen details. We pass sharp-tipped yard tools—backhoes, shovels, chainsaws—and a John Deere tractor. I trail Noah through rows of shelves stacked with coffins and caskets, zig-zagging through the cramped aisles until Noah stops.

"Here we are, Meat Wagon Number Four," Noah says with a flourish of his arm. He's pointing at my Beast, but my baby has been mutated into something awful. There are emergency lights on her roof and a ball hitch attached to her bumper. There's a white stripe running from her hood to rear, and along her side is stenciled:

J & J FUNERAL
MEAT WAGON #4

I race toward her, unhinge the back doors, and peer inside. *Fuck me.* They've morphed her guts into something that looks like a delivery van. Newly installed aluminum shelving runs floor to ceiling on either side, stretching all the way to a sheet of perforated metal that now separates the rear from the front seats. The shelves are stuffed with massive rolls of shrink-wrap, straps, tarps, and other equipment. A chrome-plated gurney rests on the floor, its legs folded underneath it.

I take a step back from my Beast. It's all too much and too sudden, and my brain struggles to reconcile my emotions. I'm thrilled to see her again, but I'm in utter miserable disbelief at her makeover. My Beast is no longer mine. She belongs to Jim. She's a meat wagon!

Noah jingles my old keys in the air as if I were some kind of pet. "Well, just don't stand there," he says, grinning. "Get in. I'm driving." I grit my teeth.

From the passenger seat, I survey the Beast's now upgraded interior with dismay. They've replaced her instrument panel with an LCD. All along the edge of the screen are odd buttons and colorful switches, and both the tachometer and speedometer are now digital. Her torn seats are now plush buckets with lumbar support and electronics that adjust up and down. This might be an upgrade to some, but for me, it's downright despicable. I'm disgusted that someone has been groping her throughout the night, changing her appearance, switching out her parts.

Noah jumps in the driver's seat and presses an orange button next to a switch. The warehouse's garage door rolls open, and morning sunbeams seep into the cab.

He twists the key in her ignition, and the Beast's familiar V8 starts up with a ferocious growl. Thank fucking goodness they haven't messed with her engine.

"So, what do you think of the fresh look?" Noah asks, smiling big-toothed.

"It's all so—"

"Cool! I know." Fuck you, Tom Petty.

"I was going to say it's different, but how? Who did all this work in one night?"

"Jim is a miracle man. I swear the guy never sleeps." Noah brings his face closer to the dash and says, "Check this out." He clears his throat. "Samantha, this is Meat Wagon Number Four. Route us to our pickup location."

A female AI voice replies through the Beast's speakers, "Certainly. Hold on while I retrieve your information." The screen transforms into a map of Whatcom County, and there's a pin dropped northwest of downtown Bellingham. The AI, Samantha, says, "Brookfield Senior Living. 5671 Buxton Lane. Six point three miles away. Thirteen minutes from your current location."

"Thanks Samantha," Noah says. He flicks a switch, triggering a tsunami siren bellowing from the Beast. Flashing multicolored lights strobe against the interior of the warehouse.

I'm heartbroken. The Beast is now a stranger, and fucking Noah is driving her. Fuck, she doesn't even smell the same. She no longer has her familiar musty stench that I've grown accustomed to. She smells like French vanilla, like a cheap European whore.

Noah revs the engine and glances at me with a smirk. "How's she sound?" he asks me.

Is he taunting me? Fucking with me like a school bully? If he's trying to break me down, it's working. He's tugging on me where it hurts. Maybe he's banking that I do something regrettable, something that he can report to Jim. Is that how this asshole gets his kicks? Fucking tattletale piece of shit. I don't trust him as far as I can throw him. So for now, I stay quiet and keep my thoughts to myself. As much as I'd like to kick him out of my driver's seat, I can't let this guy bother me. He *owns* me for the moment, so I'll play along. "She sounds great."

"You bet your ass she does. Now you better buckle up," Noah says, then we take off like a jet. He burns rubber down the driveway and takes the roundabout without hitting the brakes. We fly past the J & J gate and tear into the main street. The combination of high-pitched sirens, flashing lights, and the roaring engine wracks my nerves. We're a speeding black bullet. I had no fucking clue the Beast could move this fast.

Samantha commands Noah when and where to turn. Like duet dancers on a stage, they're in perfect sync with each other.

Samantha says, "Right at the next signal."

Noah twists the wheel going fifty.

"Left on Fargo."

Noah speeds around a curve, and tires squeal on the asphalt.

"Oh man! This meat wagon has some pep in her, doesn't she?" he shouts with glee.

I want to insist to Noah that her name is the Beast, but I also need him to focus on the road and not kill us both, so I keep my answer short with a simple "Yep."

"This job is nonstop, Max. I haven't taken a day off in months. And now, with this HIT thing killing people, work has been busy."

"Left at the fork," says Samantha.

Noah jerks the steering wheel and the Beast skids around a corner. I grab the oh-shit bar above the passenger-side window as the tires peel across the blacktop. What's with this guy? Doesn't he know anything about physics? Inertia? Traffic safety? I want to slap him and tell him, *Slow down, numb-nuts!* But I resist because this all feels like a test. He is either messing with me or fucking insane.

I keep my voice steady and ask, "Noah, who are we picking up?"

Without missing a beat he hollers, "Samantha! Who's on our pick-up list?"

She spits out a quick response. "Timothy Miller. Male. Born January third, 1946. Three hundred and fifty pounds. Brown eyes and gray hair. Caucasian. Cause of death, cardiac arrest."

Noah glances at me and says, "She knows everything about everyone."

The Beast drifts into the oncoming lane. I yell, "Watch out!"

Noah casually corrects the path, avoiding a near head-on collision. He continues, "This should be a big payday for us."

Pay? Jim said nothing about money.

"Oh yeah? How so?" I ask.

"The heavier the stiff, the more money we get, kinda like UPS. Shipping companies calculate their prices per pound. More weight, extra work. Extra work, more money. We do the same."

"Makes sense." In a fucked-up, morbid kind of way.

Noah grips the wheel with both hands—*about fucking time*—and says, "One thing you gotta understand, dead bodies are precious merchandise. They bruise easily, and with every passing hour after death, temperatures drop dramatically. That's when rigor mortis kicks in. Muscles stiffen. Blood coagulates. Hands and feet are the first to go, and when that happens, it makes it a lot harder to handle them, so we need the bodies back to the warehouse as fast as possible."

Samantha says, "In half a mile, keep left."

Noah carries on, and now he's doing his Bowie voice again, a deeper voice with a stiff delivery. "Body movers need to be quick. Sluggish pace leads to the decay of our cargo and disappoints Jim. We must also exhibit efficiency in all we do. Our aim is to secure the remains with speed and caution. We body movers use our equipment to accomplish this task, with the gurney as our key tool—"

"Turn right!" Samantha yells, her volume up.

The Beast jerks and I hold on for life. When we level out Noah asks, "Have you ever used a gurney before?" He takes one hand off the wheel.

"Never." *Put your hand back on the wheel, dummy.*

"I'll teach you and you'll be fine. Now hold on." Noah thumps on the gas pedal, and soon we're doubling the speed limit down a straight country road. I put my face against the side window and spot a bird soaring through the air. I wonder if it's hunting for food, or flying for the fuck of it. Or maybe my feathered friend is heading south for warmer weather.

Maybe one of these days, I'll do the same.

14. An overstuffed piñata

Samantha tells us we've arrived at the Brookfield Senior Living Center. The Beast slows to a crawl and heads toward a beige building propped up at the far end of a weed-infested parking lot. When we're close, Noah pulls up near the front entrance. He checks the mirrors, taps the horn twice as if were a secret handshake, then carefully reverses into the closest parking spot to the doors. I appreciate his considerate parking. It's his sole redeeming trait in our brief time together.

"So, this is the place?" I ask.

"Yep, Brookfield Senior Living, the oldest senior center in town. Now come on, we have a corpse to move."

Damn, I almost forgot why we're here.

We hop out and walk toward the rear of the Beast. Noah opens her up. "We need the gurney," he says, gesturing at the chrome-plated body mover. "And I'm gonna teach you how to use it in three seconds. You see those rubber handles? Just grab 'em tight, lift, and pull out, and that's it. The legs will fold out automatically." Noah sounds as proud as if he'd designed it himself.

I lean inside the Beast, grip the rubber handles of the gurney, and lift. It's light for its size. I walk backward until its legs drop to the parking lot, followed by a satisfying click as they lock in place.

"Hey, you're a natural," Noah says. I can't tell if he's being facetious or what. Regardless of his intent, I find the gurney easy to maneuver. He continues, "I'm gonna find out where we're needed, so grab us two straps from inside the meat wagon, then meet me inside."

Her name is the Beast.

I climb into the rear. In the shelving newly welded to her body are dozens of labeled plastic containers organized in alphabetical order. I find the container labeled STRAPS and grab a couple. "Don't you worry, baby," I whisper soothingly to the Beast before I climb out and close the doors. "You're no meat wagon. I'm gonna get you back, I promise."

Inside, Noah stands beside a check-in counter speaking to a masked female employee. I wheel the gurney toward them. The blonde receptionist wears a cream-colored uniform that matches her mask. She types away at her computer, surrounded by a clear plexiglass box as if she were a goldfish in a tank. Noah says, "Here he is."

The lady stops typing and shoots me an unimpressed look. "So this is ya new guy?" She has a faint Jersey accent.

"Lydia, this is Max. First day on the job." Noah gestures at me with his fingers shaped like a pistol.

She nods, resuming her typing.

Noah hands me a document attached to a clipboard. "Here. You'll need to sign this legal form. It says if you get sick or injured while you're here, Brookfield is not responsible."

"And if I don't sign it?" I ask, tilting my head.

"Well, I guess you can't do your job and you're back in jail."

I straighten my head. "I don't have a choice then, do I?"

"If you're asking me, you have an obvious choice, my friend."

Friend? Fuck off, you Beast-stealing prick. I paw the clipboard and pen from his hand. "Fine." I skim through the single-page disclosure, picking up on a few eye-catching words that cause me to sweat: *death, illnesses, organ failure, not liable, HIT*. I sign and date the bottom of the document and set the clipboard on the desk.

"And the pen, smart guy," Lydia says with her hand out.

"I almost forgot, sorry, here." I pass the pen to Lydia, and she places it in a jar tagged USED next to another jar marked NEW.

"I'll need your temperatures," she says, pulling out a digital thermometer gun. She asks us to uncover our heads. Lydia centers a red laser light above my nose and as she leans toward me, I notice her eyes are bloodshot and there's makeup oozed into her mask, creating splotches around the upper fold that resemble a Rorschach inkblot. The thermometer beeps.

"Poy-fect," she says with relief. "A tad above ninety-eight."

Lydia aims the tool at Noah's head. The thermometer beeps and Lydia says, "Wonderful." She resumes her seat. "Sue is expectin' you. You'll find her through the doors and down the hall. You know where to go, Noah."

A set of double doors next to her station reads STAFF ONLY. Beyond the doors, we head down a long hallway the color of lima beans beneath intermittently flickering fluorescent lights. The gurney's casters rattle over the chipped tiles, sounding like a busted grocery cart.

At Room 9 the door is ajar, and inside I glimpse a nurse sponge bathing a weeping resident. At Room

13 the door is wide open, exposing an elderly man lying on a bed hooked up to a machine, thrashing his limbs as if high-voltage electricity were running through him. Jesus H. Fucking Christ. What kind of place is this? More beeps, grunts, and human moans suffuse this forsaken hallway, creating a hellish soundtrack. I'm having second thoughts. Third and fourth thoughts too. I can't do thi—

A door bursts open and a woman in a white nurse's uniform and face mask appears. She's roughly the same age and height as my mother, middle-aged and around five foot three. She asks, her tone clipped, "J & J Funeral?"

Noah replies, "Yes, ma'am."

The nametag on her uniform reads SUE. Sue says, "Let me take you to him."

We follow Sue, and when we pass rooms 31, 33, 44, the hallway darkens and cools. The abrupt change reminds me of when once, I'd snorkeled past the Pacific ocean shelf. I remember how the seabed had dropped out from under me into a black chasm. For a moment, I'd felt this terrible sinking feeling, as if I'd gone out too far and would never return to the safety of the shore. I hadn't liked it then, and trust me, I don't fucking like it now.

"Here we are," she says outside Room 59. "Timothy Miller. Gentlemen, if you need help, ask anyone with one of these." She points at her nametag.

"Thanks Sue, but we should be fine," Noah says.

"We need this room ASAP, so by any means necessary—"

"AAAHAHHHHHAHAHH!"

My head whips around to the harrowing screams of what sounds like someone under torture from a blowtorch. Fuck this place.

I look back, and Sue is already halfway down the hallway. It occurs to me that Sue and I hadn't exchanged a single word with each other. The thought makes me feel incredibly invisible and small inside. Had she even noticed me? Is this what it feels like when you're gone? When I'm finished, expired, deceased, passed away, pushing daisies, checked out, departed, lifeless, inanimate, extinguished, perished, *six feet under, fucking dead. You, me, all of them, all of you, dead.*

"It's game time," Noah says. We zip up our face covers. Sweating, I try to take a deep breath, but the air trapped inside the suit is thin. Fuck, I can't let Noah see me freak out like this on the first day on the job. It's just a body, Max. It's just a human who once was alive, like me. *Me. Him. Dead. We're all going to be six feet deep and there's nothing we can do about it—nothing we can do about it—nothing we can do about it—fuck!* I don't think I can take another step forward. I'm done. Finito. Screw this, I'd rather go to jail than—

"Come on Max, we don't have all day." Noah beckons at me from the now-open door. *Fuck. Fuck. Fuck.* I take one more choked breath before shoving the gurney inside Room 59 and shutting the door behind me.

The room is *dead* quiet. You could almost call it tranquil. There aren't any machines beeping or patients screaming bloody murder. Hell, there's even a large window letting in natural light. This isn't too bad, aside from a terrible odor.

From the doorway, I can't see Timothy or Noah; there's a room divider blocking my line of sight. What I do see is Timothy's patient chart clipped to the divider. It reads:

Name: Timothy Miller
Sex: Male DOB: 01/03/1946
Weight: 350 Eyes: Brown Hair: Gray
Race: Caucasian
Blood type: O-
COD: Unknown

Unknown?

"Hey Max! I need you over here," Noah hollers from behind the divider.

I navigate the gurney toward the back of the room and find Noah standing above a body I assume to be Timothy, lying on a wood-frame bed. A sheet covers the body from the throat down, and all I can see is his watermelon-sized head. I walk closer and my legs shake.

Timothy's eyes are bulging out of his skull like a fish dragged from water. His mouth is unlatched, displaying foul, worn-down teeth. The skin of his face is ten shades of gray. His chins—plural—melt into his body like drippings from a wax candle. Oddly, Timothy's body seems tiny compared to his enormous melon.

"This ain't no three hundred-fifty pounder, more like two and some change," Noah says, sounding cross as if he's been cheated. He crooks his eyebrows at me. "Well, let's get down to business."

Noah tears the sheet from Timothy, and my stomach churns. Timothy's no two-hundred-whatever-pounder. Nor even three-fifty. From what I can see, he's more like five hundred. He's so enormous that his weight has splintered the wooden slats of his bed, causing his mattress to collapse to the floor. His hippo-sized torso is drum-tight like an overstuffed piñata, ready to rip at the seams from the smack of a stick. Timothy is the largest human I've ever seen, dead or alive.

The worst part is that he's naked, well, all except mercifully his groin, which is covered with a piss-yellow bath towel held together around the waist with tape. I guess they couldn't find undies big enough to fit him.

"Cha-ching. That's what I'm talking about," Noah says, excited. Positively ecstatic, he skips toward our body hauler and beckons me over. He shows me how to lower the side gate then lock the casters. That part's easy enough. But how the fuck are we going to move him?

As if reading my mind, Noah says, "We're gonna lasso a strap behind his shoulders. Then we'll pull and try to get his back off the floor. And if we can't, there's always plan B."

It sounds implausible, but I nod obediently. What the fuck do I know about moving a body?

Together, we lasso Timothy with the straps. He smells horrible and his skin feels like three-day-old fried chicken skin—loose, rotten, and oily. I'm about to lose it—*breathe*. Noah calls out, "One, two, three, pull!" The straps tighten like guitar strings, but Timothy doesn't budge. Noah barks, "Keep pulling!" But the big guy doesn't move an inch. He's heavy as a boulder. Sweat drips out my pores, soaking the inside of my suit.

"Forget it," Noah says. "Plan B it is." He ties a strap in a square knot around Timothy's ankles, then grabs the slack. He walks toward the window, opens it, and tosses the loose end through.

"Stay here, I'll be right back," he tells me, then

walks out the door with the gurney. And now it's just me and Timothy.

I've had about enough up close and personal experiences with the big guy, so I back myself to a wall, squat down, and tilt my head toward the ceiling. It's popcorn-textured and painted pale cream; if I squint, I can see hundreds of puffy clouds. That's a pleasant sight. But soon, the clouds cease to amuse me. I'm exhausted, and Timothy isn't much of a talker. My eyelids droop, and the clouds darken.

The roar of an engine snaps me to my feet.

I stand and shove my face to the window, and there's Noah climbing out of the Beast. He unlatches her rear doors, pulls out the gurney, and scoots it below me. He then grabs the loose end of the strap dangling out the window and ties it to the Beast's newly installed ball hitch.

"Stand clear!" Noah shouts at me, jumping behind the wheel. He gives her gas and the Beast lunges forward. The strap tightens and yanks Timothy out of the bed by his ankles. He skids across the floor, leaving behind a snail trail of piss and shit and bringing to light the source of the room's stench. Tires screech against the pavement, and Timothy slides feet first through the window, plopping onto the awaiting gurney outside. *Any means necessary.*

"Help me get him in," Noah snaps.

I crawl out the window and help Noah untie the strap at both ends. Noah pushes a button in the back of the Beast, and a hydraulic lift shoots out from underneath the rear doors and lowers to the ground. To the gurney's credit, it hasn't sagged in the slightest under Timothy. We push it onto the lift then collapse its legs, and with a flick of a switch the lift goes up and slides Timothy inside.

"Easy peasy," Noah tells me once we're back in the front seats. He shifts the transmission into drive. "One down, many to go. Samantha, send me the next pickup location."

"Certainly." The screen zooms into a map of Whatcom County with a pin dropped dead center on Oak Falls.

15. Shiver of Sharks

Noah tears through the mountain roads of eastern Whatcom County, hell-bent on reaching the next body in a town I dread above all: Oak Falls. His gloved fingers grip the wheel as he cuts around corners like he's racing for pole position at the Indy 500. The stinky mess in the back is contaminating the air inside the Beast, the vile stench seeping into my nostrils.

At this point, I don't have the energy to care. I've already hit my limit with this job. I need to get the fuck out of here, pronto, but first I must reclaim my Beast. I ask myself what's stopping me from yanking my keys from Noah.

Yeah, why not?

After we park, I could demand that he hands them over, and if Noah dares to resist, I'm sure I could take his sorry ass to the ground and—

What the hell am I talking about?

I'm not a fighter. Hell, I've never been in a single tussle my whole life. I'm all talk, with most of my shit-talking done inside my head. There has to be a non-violent way, but how?

I can't think straight, so for the moment I put a pause on scheming up a take-my-Beast-back-and-get-the-hell-out-of-here plan. No matter how much I hate this rapidly approaching town of Oak Falls and that I'm inches from a fucking dead body, I have to wait for the perfect moment to strike. I'll have one shot; if I screw it up, I'll be Beastless forever.

"Oak Falls is two miles ahead," Samantha tells us, her voice irritatingly smooth like a hotel switchboard operator.

Why don't you fuck off, Samantha?

I need Noah to trust me, then I'll make my move.

Thankfully, I'm a master of small talk. Asking simple questions is a skill I perfected during months of caring for my mother. Before the state took her away, she was in a childlike state of mind. Our conversations were simple and often on a loop: *Did you have a nice lunch, Mom? Have you brushed your teeth, Mom? Do you know who I am, Mom?*

"Noah, can I ask you something?"

He tenses up. "Is it personal or business?"

"Personal."

He says, "Go ahead, shoot."

"Do you have any family?"

He shakes his head. "No. They're all gone."

"None?"

"Just Jim. We're not related, but he's kept a roof over my head. Keeps me fed. You could say he's kind of my family."

You sound more like a pet than family. "That's nice of Jim. So, you must like your job."

"Why do you ask?"

"Well, I would imagine that most people don't have the stomach to handle this kind of work, and you seem to have a real knack for it. So, what turns your gears about working as a body mover?"

Noah releases one hand from the steering wheel and scratches the back of his neck, thinking for a moment before he responds. "I enjoy being on call, ready to run out the door at a moment's notice. It's like I'm a firefighter, but instead of saving people from burning buildings, I move the ones they *don't* save. Someone has to, right? People die, and it's my job to haul them away. It's essential work."

"Yeah, I guess so."

Samantha chimes in, "Your destination is up ahead. Oak Falls, Washington State."

Oh shut up, Samantha. Like I needed a reminder.

The Nonessentials

As we narrow in toward our target, our majestic view of Cascadian evergreens and snow-capped Mount Baker becomes superimposed by moss-covered trailers as far as the eye can see. Rusted-out cars abandoned in all directions. Heaps of trash and broken glass littered on the streets. Packs of stray dogs roaming about, barking, pissing, scratching their flea-bitten skin. And the occasional resident stumbling out from whatever hole they came from, bottle in one hand, smoke in the other. *Welcome to Oak Falls, ladies and gentlemen.*

Small talk.

"So, how often are you here picking up bodies in Oak Falls?" I try my best to sound as sincere and interested as possible.

Noah doesn't answer. Instead, he slams on the brakes.

In front of us are three skinny kids, circling the road lazily on rust-red Schwinn cruisers. Seemingly oblivious to the collision they almost caused, they continue to pedal slowly, never stopping, always moving, like a shiver of sharks in open water surrounding their prey.

I can tell Noah's contemplating if he should mow through them, but after a moment he beats the horn and yells, "Move it or lose it, you three!"

The sharks shove aside and we drive past them. I notice the tallest kid with a wispy mustache shaking his ginger head and squinting his bright blue orbs at us. Fuck, it's the same pasty shits who maced me.

"Those little shits," Noah mumbles. "To answer your question, Max, I'm here all the time. This is my third trip since yesterday."

"*Third?* When do you sleep?"

"This job won't let you sleep. We're on call for a solid seventy-two hours. Like Jim always says, you can sleep when you're dead."

"Is it extra busy here because of HIT?"

"It's been busy here long before that," Noah smirks.

Samantha: "You have arrived."

Our destination turns out to be a run-down two-story apartment building that resembles an abandoned Super 8 Motel. It's missing half its shingles and looks as if all it would take to blow the monstrosity over is a heavy breeze.

Backed in near the apartment is a squad car with the trunk raised. Noah pulls up beside it as the lid slams shut, revealing that cowboy-hat-wearing sonofabitch Sheriff Evans. Noah rolls down his window and waves.

"Morning," Evans says, approaching us. "Well, look at you, all suited up and working for the man." Evans winks at me, then focuses his attention on Noah.

"Where's the goods, Sheriff?" Noah asks, back in his fake-nice voice.

"Upstairs, and it ain't pretty. Overdose, I suspect. Stupid junkies around here never stop. Anyways Noah, any trouble with your new boy?"

Noah glances at me then says to Evans, "No trouble, Sheriff."

"Well, let's hope it keeps that way."

What's with this fucking guy Evans? He's talking about me like I'm not even here.

"I won't keep you fellas any longer. Your payload's up in 202. Now if you'll excuse me, nature calls. Play nice you two." Evans tips his hat, gets into his car, and bolts off with his emergency lights flashing.

Outside my passenger window, a chain-link fence rattles. I whip my head toward the sound and see a pair of pale hands gripping the mental links.

"Max," Noah says.

"Yeah?"

"Zip up. It's game time."

We get out and Noah unlatches the meat wag —*fuck*—the Beast's rear. We crawl in and Noah orders me to grab the corpse's legs and pull them off the gurney. I do as he says but man-oh-man, even with a freaking hazmat suit on, it reeks. I can taste Timothy's rotting fumes in the back of my throat, and it makes me wonder how well the suit is working. *His death, my death. Dead. We're all going to die and there's nothing*—my knees shake and my eyelids flutter—I'm going to pass out. I slump down and face-plant on Timothy's hairy chest.

"Get up! This is no time for a nap!" Noah yells.

The following moments are a blur. In a rush of sheer disgust, I pull with strength I didn't know I possessed, rolling Timothy off to the side. We pull the gurney from the Beast and carry it, hustling toward the apartment's stairwell.

"Watch your step," Noah warns. Parts of the stairs are missing. I put my hand out to steady myself on the wooden handrail but it's no help; it's mushy, likely rotten to its core.

Making it to the second floor, we plant the gurney down, drop its wheels, and roll it up to unit 202. Next door, in unit 203, I catch an older woman staring at me from behind a window. She's wearing a fuzzy purple robe with pink curlers in her hair, and a thin cigarette hangs from her rose-painted lips. She shakes her head at me at the speed of a sloth as she exhales tobacco smoke against the glass, then walks away.

Noah pushes the door open with his shoulder. Once he has it cracked open, I can see piles of liquor bottles all over a dirty mustard-colored carpet. Noah slides in and kicks over a pile of bottles, pissing off a family of feasting flies that swarm him. He swats at the filthy things and they buzz off.

I follow, rolling the gurney over the threshold. The carpet squelches—it's soaking wet and there's black mold growing on the plaster. I step inside and to my right, there's a door jamb without a door. I poke my head through it. It's a bathroom with a smashed porcelain toilet, rusted water oozing from the tank and puddling over the linoleum floor. Between the toilet and bathtub is an empty box with the letters APM TP.

"Max! Over here," Noah calls.

As I leave the bathroom and head toward Noah's voice, something smacks me on the top of my head. Some kind of white goo slimes down the front of my face guard. What the hell? A loogie? I look up. Through the streaks on my guard, I make out a small hole in the rotted ceiling with fucking pigeons perched on its rim.

"Gross!" I yell.

Noah responds, "What is it?"

"A bird just shit on me."

He walks into view, tilts his head up, then chuckles. "Well, would you look at that? An Oak Falls skylight."

"Whatever," I grumble. I begin to wipe off my mask but my suit's rubber gloves make it worse, smearing the bird shit even more.

Noah reaches into his pocket and hands me a moist wipe packet. "Here, use this. Some say when a bird craps on your head, it's a sign of good luck."

"Funny, I don't *feel* lucky." I clumsily tear apart the packet and wipe off the shit.

"Well, you should. Look, we got a double banger."

I follow Noah into a hillbilly crank kitchen. Scattered across the floor and countertop are random funnels, glass jars, powders, a digital scale, and five-gallon buckets filled with pale yellow pulp. Past the kitchen is a living room with a torn floral-patterned sofa. Beside it are two bodies tangled together, lying face-down.

Noah taps my shoulder. "It's showtime." He walks toward the bodies and flips one over, and fuck me if it isn't that red-headed mullet bastard. Mr. Mullet was alive and well some twenty-four hours ago, and now he looks like he's been dead for days, his skin an awful shade of green and covered with pus-filled blisters. Dead from what?

"Do they have HIT?" I ask.

"No. Sheriff said overdose." Noah stares at the bodies for a moment then adds in a hushed voice, "But double check if your suit is zipped all the way up."

Noah turns over body number two. It's a woman, also a ginger. Girlfriend, wife, sister, daughter? No idea. It's hard to tell the age of a face with dried puke splattered all over it.

"Look at that," Noah says. There's a black leather belt wrapped around her throat, along with minor cuts and bruises all over her face as if a cat has mauled her. I'm not a homicide detective, but this is a fucking weird-looking overdose scene.

Noah says, "You think you can handle two at a time?"

They look like hell, but they don't seem heavy—she's a hundred pounds if that, and Mr. Mullet is maybe a buck-fifty. "Sure, why not."

We kick the piles of trash out of our path, then I roll the gurney close to the red-headed stiffs and lower it flat to the floor. Noah grabs Mr. Mullet's arms, I get a hold of his feet, and together we shove him aboard and toss his girlfriend on top. Compared to Timothy, handling these two feels like lifting grocery bags.

Noah says, "Up on three. One, two, three." We lift the gurney until the legs click into place. I lead the way out of the apartment, moving backward, and pause at the top of the stairs outside. Once Noah's ready, I take my first step down with the gurney white-knuckled in both hands. My foot plants down. The stair feels solid enough, so I shift my weight and take another step.

"You okay?" Noah asks.

"Doing fi—" My foot falls through a rotten

board and I fall backward. I grab the handrail with one hand but it crumbles beneath my fingers and I keep falling. The gurney slips away from me. Noah tries to keep his hold on it, but it rips from his hands and rattles past me down the remaining stairs. With two loud thuds, the bodies tumble to the cement like crash test dummies.

Noah rushes down, passing me. "Our merchandise!" he yells. "Get up and help me!"

My foot's still stuck in the rotted step. My ankle throbs but I can wriggle it. By the time I've freed myself and reached him, Noah already has the girl back on the gurney. I help him with Mr. Mullet, then we push them toward the Beast. We shove them next to Timothy, nearly doubling the size of our flesh pile.

Once we're back in the cab, Noah says we need to haul ass back to the warehouse. "Samantha! Map us home," he commands.

"Certainly." The LCD screen illuminates a map with a drop pin. "Your estimated arrival time is seventeen minutes."

"Nope," Noah says. "We're getting there in eight."

16. Circle of Trust

Noah asks me to check on our precious cargo. With a sigh, I swivel in my seat and peer through the perforated holes in the metal wall separating us from them. Timothy's at the bottom serving as a squishy foundation while on top of him, Mr. and Mrs. Mullet's limp appendages sway with each quick turn of the Beast. It's a dreadful sight like some twisted version of that old grade school game Dogpile except here, Timothy won't ever get the chance to yell, "You win, now get off me!"

"They're fine," I inform Noah.

He flips a switch that triggers sirens and lights. The Beast's RPMs redline and we haul ass, running through red lights and dodging traffic cones along with the occasional chunk of tire carcass. I want to scream at him, *Chill the fuck out! What's the fucking rush?* Instead I remain quiet as the Dogpile behind us thumps against the metal wall. I could really use a fucking zap.

Samantha says the magic words: "You have arrived."

Noah drives past the J & J gate and whips around the roundabout without using the brakes. Once we're within eyeshot of the warehouse, he pushes a button on the dash and the garage door rolls up. He checks the mirrors, honks twice, then backs her in.

"Solid work back there," he tells me, killing the engine. "You're a natural."

I shrug and jump out of my seat. As we make our way toward the rear of the Beast, I hear hands clapping. I look over and it's Jim striding toward us, and he's not alone. There's a guy beside him, and he's built like a brick house: no neck, broad shoulders, arms as big as my legs. He's wearing a bloody rubber apron over his barrel chest.

Jim stops clapping and says, "There they are. Our fearless body movers. Tell me boys, how was it? Did everyone play nice?"

I haven't seen Jim since jail, and I'd forgotten how tall he is.

Noah says, hands resting at his hips, "This guy is a keeper, Boss."

"Wonderful," Jim says, then cracks his knuckles. "Maxwell, how does it feel to be an *essential* worker?"

How do I feel? All day I've felt nauseated and on the verge of mental collapse, and I would be perfectly fine if I never touched another stinking body for the rest of my fucking life.

I say, "I'm grateful, Boss, for the opportunity."

"Grateful?" Jim turns his face to that brick house at his side. "Did you hear that, Junior? *Grateful,* he says. I told you this one is special in more ways than one."

Jim takes a step closer to the Beast and runs a finger along her new racing stripes while he says, "You know, Maxwell, I spent a small fortune on your Suburban, so be honest with me. Do you like what I've done?"

You turned my Beast into a freak. And you had the gall to stamp your company name on her. Meat wagon number four?

I look at Jim straight-faced and tell him, "Boss, she's never looked better."

Jim erupts into a crazed laughing fit, then smacks his thigh and says, "Hot damn. I knew I'd like you, Maxwell. I'm tickled that you *approve* of the transformation. I can't tell you enough how great it is to have you on team J & J. Oh, which reminds me, allow me to introduce you to a key player around here—Junior."

Jim points at the brick house as if he were a

prize on *The Price Is Right*. Junior is emotionless, stiff, and I don't see him blink once. "Get over here," Jim says in a commanding voice. "I want you to meet Maxwell. He's our newest body mover."

Junior lets out a weird moan and shuffles over. Jim continues, "Junior is our muscle around here. He'll offload whatever you two bring back."

"Nice to meet you, Junior."

Junior's eyes are like two giant black saucers. They roll toward the ceiling, and he emits a grunt. A moment of awkward silence passes. Jim coughs, rubs his hands together, and says, "Now that we're all properly acquainted, let's see what you two have for me."

Noah swings the Beast's back doors open and Jim counts out loud, "One, two, three bodies for me? Fan-fuckin'-tastic. Looks like six or seven hundred pounds of flesh. Not a terrible morning if I do say so myself. Now Junior, get these three money bags weighed, tagged, and processed for me while I'm gone."

Junior grunts, then treads toward a four-wheeled handcart like you'd see at Costco and rolls it up to the Beast. With one hand, he drags Mr. Mullet out from the back and onto the Costco cart as if he weighed nothing.

"Noah," Jim says.

"Yes, Boss?"

"Could you be a gent and escort Maxwell to the break room? You guys should fuel up before heading back out."

"Sure thing, Boss, thanks."

"And Maxwell, when you're full, have Noah bring you to my office. There's something that we need to sort out."

I don't like the sound of that. I nod and Jim walks away, whistling to the tune of "We're in the Money."

Noah and I leave Junior with the bodies and make our way through the warehouse. We pass by an open toolbox, and lying inside it is a familiar wood-handled screwdriver—it's the one that Carter gifted me. Without stopping to think, I grab the tool and shove it inside my hip pocket. Noah doesn't notice.

The break room is down the main hallway, only a few doors from my sleeping quarters. Inside is a black leather sofa, a split-door refrigerator, and a square wooden table piled high with treats that look like contraband from a kid's birthday party—train-themed cupcakes and bite-sized candies.

Noah barrels toward the refrigerator and tears it open. It's loaded with kids' juices and sodas. He paws an orange juice box and stabs it with a straw.

"What is all this?" I ask, watching Noah suck down the sugary liquid.

"Lunch, duh. Have as much as you like."

"I mean, where did all *this* come from?" I gesture at the birthday party treats.

Noah crushes his juice box, tosses it in a trashcan, and grabs a second.

"A funeral service, where else?" he says. "Here, look for yourself."

He walks toward a small pile of pamphlets resting on the sofa's armrest and hands one to me. On the cover is a black-and-white portrait of a kid with a gap-toothed smile and hair parted neatly to one side. Print above his head reads:

SAMUEL S. GREENHORN
A CELEBRATION OF LIFE

Noah sets down his drink and snatches a choo-choo-train cupcake from the table. He chomps down on the treat then says with his mouth full, "Perks of the job." He swallows and says, "We don't get too many kids' funerals. If you ask me, they taste better."

My stomach makes a queasy sound. Noah throws his hands up in the air. "I can hear your gut rumbling from here. We're off the clock so go ahead, eat something."

He's right, I'm starving. I try not to look at Samuel's face as I grab his funeral cupcake and bite off a small piece. It's delicious and I end up devouring the remaining chunk in one gulp. My mouth full of sticky, gooey choo-choo goodness, I walk over to the fridge and wash the cupcake down with cherry soda. I repeat this process, stuffing children's sweets down my throat and gulping soda until I'm pleasantly stuffed. I plop my ass on the leather sofa to digest. I sigh as my aching body sinks into the comfortable cushions. Who knew moving bodies would be so exhausting?

"Feeling better?" Noah asks, his mouth crammed with cheddar crackers.

I wipe frosting from the corners of my lips. "Much."

Many burps later, Noah says it's time to take me to Jim's office. He leads me down the main hallway. This time, instead of going toward the warehouse, we hang left through a spacious cathedral room. In the room are burgundy-cushioned chairs arranged in a row, facing a wooden casket surrounded by bouquets of flowers. Suddenly, I'm a little boy again in the front row beside my crying mother. A pastor stands above my father's casket saying how unfair and fragile life can be—

"It's down here," Noah says.

Snapping out of it, I follow Noah to an arched wooden door with a brass knocker. Noah says he'll catch up with me later and walks away. I reach for the knocker and give the door a couple of taps. I hear Jim's voice beckoning me in.

His office is spacious with two narrow windows overlooking the front gate, and in the center of the room is Jim. He sits on an oversized leather chair behind a mahogany desk that holds up an outdated beige PC, a cordless phone, loose papers, and a thick book. I scan the book's spine: *The Gravedigger's Handbook, Volume III*. Three chairs face him.

Jim instructs me to sit. I take the middle of the three chairs and wait patiently for him to continue. Leaning forward over his desk and staring at me intensely, he makes a tiny circle in the air with his index finger. "Do you know what this is, Maxwell?"

"Uh, a circle?"

"Close. It's my circle of trust. This circle is unbreakable if we're honest with one another. Noah and Junior are part of this circle, and I would like it if you were as well because the greater the circle, the richer and more powerful we have the potential to become." As he talks, Jim continues to sketch a circle in front of him, its circumference steadily growing larger until he's swinging his arm around like a windmill.

Jim stops and opens a drawer near his knees, grabs something, and says, "Truth." He then sets my confiscated vial of aloe vera concentrate on his desk. "Tell me Maxwell, where did you get this?"

I remember that I already told Deputy

Asshole that I found it. I've got to keep my story straight. "I just found it. It was lying on the sidewalk near Holly Street," I explain, keeping my inflection steady.

Jim raises his eyebrows. "What compelled you to pick it up?"

"No reason, I just took it. Why, what is it?"

"It's just something that I've been needing for a while." Jim sets the vial aside. "So, I had my forensics team run some tests on this. They discovered two sets of prints. One is yours, and the second belongs to a girl named Sunshine Harlow."

Jim lifts a piece of paper from a stack on his desk. It's a mugshot of Sunshine, and she's holding up a case number. *What the fuck!*

"I'm going to ask this just once, Maxwell. Do you know this girl?"

I feel my blood boiling through my veins. I'm going to combust. *Breathe*. If he knows I'm lying, I'm done for.

"Jim, I've never met that person before in my life."

Jim stares at me, biting his bottom lip, then opens a desk drawer and slides Sunshine's mugshot into it. "Okay then," he says. "Now that we have that cleared up, where were we? Right!"

Jim fumbles through a stack of documents on his desk and hands me a sheet titled New Hire Form, along with a J & J-branded ballpoint pen.

"Maxwell, I know you've just started here, but to be perfectly honest you've already outlasted others before you, so I'd like to propose something to you. Okay? Once Phase Zero is over and your work release is completed, what do you say about joining my staff full time? You'll get paid handsomely for your efforts, plus all the—"

Jim's office phone rings and he glances at the caller ID. "I gotta take this." He stands with the cordless phone earpiece held tight to his ear. "Tell me, how many—"

He walks out into the hallway, the door shuts, and now it's solely me inside his office. I hear his voice trailing off as he ambles down the hall, talking to whoever is on the phone. Like a spring, I jump out of my chair and ravage through Jim's desk, looking for information about what, if anything, they've done with Sunshine.

I find her mugshot in the top drawer. Her hair is shorter in it. It's clear that it's an old photo of her. Written on it is her name, age, and vital statistics, and nothing else. I set it aside. Also in the drawer is a photo of a much younger Jim. He's in a tuxedo and standing next to his bride, cutting a wedding cake. I flip it over, and in handwritten ink it says: Jim & Jane, July 13th, 2002.

I set the pictures back in the drawer, close it, then tug on the drawer below it, but it's locked.

When I crouch down, a sharp pain stabs me in my leg—Carter's screwdriver.

I glance over at the office door, then back to the drawer, then back to the door again. Yanking the screwdriver from my pocket, I jam its sharp end inside the drawer's lock and twist. The lock pops. "Never leave home without it," I mutter, hearing Carter's voice in my head. Inside is a thick manila folder with the words PHASE ZERO PROTOCOLS stamped red on the cover.

I hear Jim's voice, and my skin goosebumps. I shove the folder inside my hazmat suit, slam the drawer closed, and scramble back to my chair.

The door opens. "Sorry about that. Business. There's always something." Jim returns to his position behind the mahogany desk and shoves the new hire document and a pen at me. "So Maxwell, how about it? Are you gonna join the winning team?"

I'll do whatever it takes to get out of here. "I sure am, Boss." I take the pen from Jim, pretend to read over the document, and scrawl an illegible signature on the dotted line.

He takes the form and says, "Fan-fucking-tastic." We shake and I head out. As I'm nearing the exit, Jim says, "Wait one second."

Fuck, he's noticed the broken lock. I turn, thumper beating against my ribs.

"Will you let Noah know that you guys have

three more stiffs to pick up at Brookfield? They're dropping like flies over there."

Panic fades as I exhale in relief. "I sure will, Boss."

Jim makes a little circle motion with his finger, and I mirror his movement like a dope before slipping out the door.

17. Out of sight

I'm a fuzz of motion as I push my body to its absolute limits, tearing through the hallway faster than you can say lickety-split. I have one thought on my mind: Get the fuck out of here. Boss-man will soon catch wind of the breach in his precious trust circle, and when he does, I want to be as far away from him and his crew as possible.

The damn folder I've crammed in my suit has sunk down to my thigh and it might as well be barbed wire because it's slicing the insides of my legs, but I can't stop. There's no tapping out, no easing up, not here, not now, not until I'm safe inside my Beast.

By a stroke of luck, I don't run into Noah, Junior, or anyone else in the halls to impede my path, and soon I'm face to face with my ticket to freedom, the door leading into the warehouse. I lunge at the handle, and my hopes crash and burn. I should've expected this. It's locked.

My screwdriver won't be any help against this solid steel door since there's not even a keyhole to jam it in. Unlocking the numeric keypad is my only way out. My fingers desperately hammer down a random three-digit sequence. A red light flashes, accompanied by a buzz that somehow sounds disappointed in me. *Shit.* I try again, another random sequence. Eight, five, and—

"MAXWELL!"

My body jolts from the keypad as Jim's voice crackles through the air, smoldering with enough anger to melt rock. My pulse quickens and my vision blurs, but with a steady inhale, I return to the damn numeric puzzle. Time seems to stretch, each second a day as I stare at the buttons, and then I see it. A trio of numbers stands out, their surfaces worn by countless finger taps: three, seven, and nine.

Jim's roar slices through the air again. "Maxwell! Where are you?!"

"Come on," I mutter, silent calculations churning in my head. There's a method to this madness, a mathematical code to crack. Without repeating any numbers, there's six combinations of three, seven, and nine. I slam in a potential sequence, a sharp punch to the three followed by the seven and nine. Bzzzzz! The crimson eye of the keypad blinks back at me defiantly.

I don't let frustration get to me. I move onto the next, fingers moving rhythmically. Three, nine, seven. A red flash and a buzz. The seconds keep ticking by and there's no time for doubt, no space for hesitation. Jim's closing in.

"You broke our circle, Maxwell!" Jim hollers, nearer than ever. His foot-stomping shakes the wooden floorboards beneath me. "Where do you think you're going? I *own* you!"

I swivel around and there's Jim, a storm cloud personified, his fists balled up like he's ready to rain down hell. His question hangs in the air, but I'm not giving up anything—not a word. A savage grin curls my lips as fingers dance across the keypad again, a sequence born of sheer desperation—seven, three, nine. Red. This is as disappointing as a flat tire on a getaway car.

"The protocol documents. Hand them over!"

I'm shaking and sweating, but I swallow the pressure as if it were liquid courage. I take a deep breath, and then, like a daydream, a memory of the sausage-like fingers of Sheriff Evans pops into my mind, punching in numbers on the J & J gate as I watch from the back seat.

Nine. Three. Seven.

I punch in the combo.

Bingo. Green light and a high-pitched beep.

The deadbolt retracts.

"Maxwell, I know where you fucking live!" Jim's running at me as I yank the door open, dart through, and slam the door in his face. Across the warehouse I see her, my Beast. She's parked beside the roll-up door. I run toward her, seize the screwdriver from my pocket, jump inside the cab, tell her I'm sorry, then stab the steel tip deep into her ignition. I twist the tool and the Beast roars to life.

I shut the door and lock it. Two heartbeats pass and Jim and Junior have surrounded me on both sides. Jim screams, "Get out of my meat wagon!" as he tries to open the doors. Junior has a lead pipe clenched in his hand, and he beats it against her passenger door.

BAM! BAM!

Which button opens this goddamn garage door? I don't remember so I press all the buttons, and now the Beast's alarm is blaring, and the lights are flashing—

"Stop!" Jim yells.

My throat is so dry I can't swallow. Then I remember that there might be one entity who can get me out of this jam. "Samantha. Help me, please." My voice comes out as a croak.

Samantha responds, cheerful as ever, "How can I help you today?"

"Open the garage door."

"I can't help you with your request."

"This is an emergency, Samantha! Please, I need to get out of here."

Samantha goes quiet for a moment, and I'm afraid I've lost her. Then she says, "If this is an emergency, I suggest you drive through the door."

Why didn't I think of that?

The Beast roars with unleashed power as she leaps forward and into the roll-up door. It crumbles like shattered dreams as its hardware falls from the ceiling. I press on. The Beast's V8 is a symphony of raw, untamed power. My heartbeats sync with the engine's rumble, and it's at this moment I'm reminded of the iron gate guarding my escape.

FUCK IT!

Forty miles per hour becomes sixty as the asphalt races past beneath me. Both hands gripping the wheel as I hammer the gas pedal to the floor, I brace for impact.

WHAM!

The Beast's steel bumper crashes into the gate like a battering ram, smashing it from its hinges and sending it flying across the pavement. We're through. I can't stop myself from laughing. My eyes water as I spew sounds of joy and relief. I can't recall ever feeling so alive. I keep the Beast above sixty, not letting off the gas until J & J is out of sight.

18.
Double-palm stop

The further I distance myself from Jim and his dim-witted crew, the steadier my heart beats. Now that I'm miles away and feeling somewhat composed, reality crashes down and the realization of urgent matters needing attention hits me like a ton of bricks. I have to warn Sunshine that they're after her, but I don't have her phone number. I could call Carter, but they've confiscated my phone. Should I just drive there?

I pull over to the side of the road and try to think. My mind swims and I feel utterly depleted —I need a zap. One solid light session and I'll be good as new, recharged to a hundred percent. There's even an old pay phone a block from my clinic; I haven't used it in years, but maybe it's still in service. Hmm, downtown could be dodgy. Driving through in broad daylight is asking for trouble, but wait—I'm still flossin' a hazmat suit and the Beast looks legit. It's a chewy choice and every neuron in my body says go to Glacier, go north to Sunshine's, but the thing is, my clinic is practically on the way.

I dash, duck, and weave through side streets, keeping myself and the Beast unseen for as long as possible. When I reach the southern edge of downtown, I slow and gauge what I see before me. It's the aftermath of a rebellion and the government definitely won because I don't see any civilians, only an army of deputies patrolling the streets. They're all head-shaven and dressed in the familiar tan uniforms, moving in perfect unison as they march in and out of roadways in pairs. They're everywhere.

Yet I'm so close to Brighter Days, and even though it's a coin flip whether my clinic is totally looted or burned to the ground, going back isn't an option. I'm in too deep and I need a zap now more than ever, so I shove on.

On Main Street, I pass more boarded-up buildings and more patrolling deputies. They pay no attention to me, and one of them even gives me a salute. I see the pay phone booth near my clinic, but it's wrapped up with caution tape and surrounded by guards.

Before I know it, I'm on Bay Street and I can see my clinic's marquee dangling by one chain.

Unfortunately, I also see a roadblock barring my path, and standing beside it is an armed deputy. He's repeating into a megaphone, "Nobody outside until further notice. Return to your residences. Phase Zero has begun."

He sees me and lowers his megaphone to his side before walking toward the Beast. His movements are swift and calculated as he closes in. I catch him glancing at the J & J company logo, and I think to myself, *Relax Max, you look like an essential worker.* The deputy tips his hat, and I swear this guy could be my ninth-grade math teacher, Mr. Spelding. He springs a thumb up from his fist then waves me through. Well, that was easy.

As the Beast is inching past the roadblock, I catch him in my mirror snatching the radio from his hip. His hands change from waving to a double-palm stop.

"Pull over!" he demands. I brake, and he draws his shooter from his belt. "Get out of the vehicle with your hands above your head!"

I raise one hand high and unbuckle my belt cautiously with the other. The deputy lowers his weapon and trots toward me. A voice inside my head screams *DRIVE!* I stomp on the gas.

Rubber peels as the rear of the Beast glances off the roadblock and she fishtails down the street. The deputy fires shots, but misses. I keep the gas floored, not letting up once as the Beast races through town like a goddamn maniac high on speed. Fuck my clinic, I'm out of here.

"Samantha," I cry. "Take me to Glacier."

"Certainly." A map appears on the screen. "Turn around," Samantha commands.

I flip a bitch in the street, the world outside my windows a blur.

"Continue through the light," she says.

I speed through a red light, then another, maneuvering along narrow one-lane roads only to run into a group of deputies arranged in a V formation and unleashing a hail of bullets in my direction.

"Samantha, help!"

"How can I help you?

"Re-route. Now!"

"Certainly." The map changes. "Right at the fork then left onto the I-5 North," she tells me.

I rip the wheel to the right, narrowly missing a utility pole, and hurl toward the Interstate. The road up ahead is free of deputies, but my sense of victory is short-lived as two squad cars pull up behind the Beast, sirens wailing and lights flashing. They're gaining on me. One instructs me over his intercom, "Pull your vehicle over!"

No fucking way, I'm not going down again. Not now, not ever. I keep the gas pedal down as I race onto the I-5, passing exit after exit trying to outrun my tails.

I look down at the Beast's new digital speedometer, and she's moving faster than I've ever pushed her before. She's going over a hundred and still climbing, but the squad cars are still all over me.

BANG! BANG!

Gunshots fire, sirens blare, my rear view is blazing with cherries-and-berries, and I think to myself that this is how I'm going out. This is the end, me and the Beast like *Thelma and Louise*—

A smoking heap of cars up ahead blocks both northbound lanes. I hit the brakes but I'm moving too fast to stop in time so I brace for impact, hands tight around the wheel, my teeth clenched. Three, two, one—BOOM!

The Beast splits the pile of tin like a wrecking ball, and all my two-hundred-plus bones want to jolt out of my skin. Cars flip, twist, and explode all around me, yet my tires keep in contact with the asphalt. She *is* a goddamn tank.

I glance in my side mirror, and behind me it looks like the climax of a James Cameron blockbuster. The deputies lock up their brakes; their tires smoke and squeal as they try to avoid the wreckage, but they should be so lucky. The two squad cars collide and bounce off each other, flip head over tail faster than an Olympic gymnast, then explode into giant fireballs.

I slow to safer speeds, clear my throat, and tell Samantha thanks.

"My pleasure," she says.

She's growing on me.

19. After the Roundabout

I EXIT THE INTERSTATE AND DRIVE EASTBOUND on Mount Baker Highway for fuck-knows-how-long—too long—running on the last of my reserves, nothing but fumes for yours truly. It's a damn struggle to keep my eyes wide open as I split my focus to maintain all four tires on the road while looking out for any potential bogies. So far so good —I haven't encountered trouble, not one bastard deputy or roadblock. I'll chalk that up as a win, even if it is dumb luck.

"You have arrived. Glacier, Washington," Samantha says.

Glacier is home to a thousand residents, give or take, and Sunshine's place is down one of the many gravel driveways off the main drag, but for the life of me, I can't remember which one. I ask Samantha for Sunshine's address, but it's not listed. I can't call her, and I don't want to pound on random doors and ask, so I have to rely on my memory and that's limited at the moment. I slow the Beast and scan out the window. If I see her driveway, I'm sure I'll recognize it. Well, maybe.

The first handful of driveways I roll past are too wide or paved with blacktop. Nope. I continue past others with private gates and dirt roads. None are Sunshine's. This isn't working and I'm wasting precious fuel, so I pull the Beast over.

"Samantha, give me a map of my current location."

"Certainly," she says, and within a second, a crisp map of Glacier appears on the screen.

I pinch and zoom with my fingers on the map. Down the road is a community center, a corner store, a housing development in the woods—and a barn that could be hers. I zoom in and I'm able to make out a structure beside it that looks like Sunshine's house.

Just then, a flock of birds squawk overhead. They sound distressed. I look up through the windshield and peer toward the clouds. Dozens of birds are freaking out, but not from a predator. There's a twisting tornado of black smoke in the sky in the direction of that barn.

My blood runs cold and I feel a sharp pain in my gut. The last I checked, where there's smoke there's fire. *Fuck.* I must be losing my mind, because the next thing I do is drive straight toward the tornado.

The closer I get, the harder it is to see as pieces of ash impair my vision. Before long I can't see jack shit, so I flip on the windshield wipers to full speed. The wipers help, and up ahead I see a gravel driveway. I move toward it and recognize it as Sunshine's property, but it's engulfed in a giant inferno. The entire lot is ablaze, and I can feel the scorching temperature even from inside the Beast. I push forward until I can't move any further or the heat will melt the rubber around my rims.

I leap out of the cab shouting Sunshine and Carter's names but it's no use, my voice is lost in the inferno's roar. The heat cooks the skin of my face; my throat burns from the heavy smoke. I have to get out of here before the fire swallows me whole. I climb back inside the cab, feeling frantic and literally hot under the collar.

Assuming that Carter and Sunshine aren't burnt to a crisp, they could both be at Carter's father's place, Chuck's. It's been years since I've visited, and I'm not so sure I can find his home on my own.

"Samantha, can you map the home address for Chuck Jackson in Deming?"

"Certainly," she says, and the LCD screen presents two addresses:

C. Jackson, 4591 W. Crate St.

C. Jackson, 994 E. Winston St.

Fuck, what was it? Crate or Winston ... Wait ... Carter's favorite book. He loved that his street name was ...

"Samantha, who's the protagonist of George Orwell's novel *1984*?"

She answers promptly, "Winston Smith."

"Samantha, take me to 994 East Winston."

"Certainly," she says and instructs me to head west for a mile, then to take a left on Enterprise.

I pass Sid's Corner Store, home of the best hand-dipped corn dogs in town, and it's boarded up with plywood. There's a sign that says: CLOSED BY ORDER OF PHASE ZERO. I cross a set of empty train tracks, take a right on Birch Bay Way, and keep driving until I pass over the Nooksack River, which is quite low for this time of year.

Samantha tells me to continue straight. I thank her, then roll over a half dozen speed bumps before making a right on Davis, and finish the trek by hanging a left after the roundabout. Samantha tells me, "You have arrived."

I wonder if I've made a mistake. The house I see before me is unkempt, with peeling paint and an overgrown yard. The roof sags under the weight of years' worth of moss. The US flag flapping above the garage is tattered. There's nothing Chuck-like about it—that guy kept his home spotless. But it's the correct shape, a single-level with an attached garage. Could this be it? As I hesitate, old memories resurface.

I'm twelve and saying to Carter in his bedroom, "Your dad is a gladiator! He could chew me up and rip me in half if he wanted to." Carter agrees and says, "But he would never hurt a hair on your head. You're like a second son to him."

I'm in Chuck's living room with the big guy sitting next to me, regaling me with stories about jumping out of planes when he was an active Marine. The guy is twice my height and three times my weight with mighty fists, anaconda-thick arms, and a wine-barrel-sized chest.

I'm older, it's summer, and Carter and I are cheering for Chuck at an arm wrestling tournament. He wins, becoming a three-time Washington State arm wrestling champion—for both arms.

Enough reminiscing. I keep the screwdriver inside the ignition and walk toward the front entrance. I hike up a few cement steps to the door, knock, and call out, "Chuck! Carter! Is anyone home?"

Several minutes pass and nobody answers. I think about how Chuck used to always greet me at his door with his hand out for a handshake. "Max, put it here," he'd say to me, and I'd feel the power of his stone-crushing grip as we shake. I'd say,

"Great to see you, Mr. Jackson," and he'd always tell me, "Call me Chuck."

I knock again. Nothing. Feeling beaten and defeated, I shuffle back toward the Beast. I'm halfway down the driveway when I hear my name. I turn and see Carter standing inside the doorway. "What the hell are you wearing?" he shouts. "Is that a hazmat suit?"

I'd forgotten I'm sporting my body hauler getup. The outfit is quite comfortable once it's broken in.

"It's a long story, but yeah, it is."

Carter glances past me toward the Beast.

"What the fuck happened to your ride? Are those ambulance lights on the roof and racing stripes?"

"Correct again, and—"

"Max, you look like shit! Are you sick? Do you have HIT?"

"No, I don't have HIT. I'm fine, well no ... I'm not. Can I come in?"

"Of course, but be quiet. Pops is sleeping."

I meet Carter at the door with a brotherly hug. I notice that he's well-rested and calm. *Does he know about—*

"Dude," he says, "why do you smell like fire-roasted pickles?"

"I'll tell you, but first, is Sunshine with you?"

He looks at me confused and says, "I left her place yesterday. Why?"

A head rush sucker-punches me in the face. I see stars and my knees buckle. Carter tries to anchor me but I'm collapsing, the world is nose-diving into shadows, and I black out.

20. Put it here

I snap awake, dry mouthed, groggy, and sprawled out on Chuck's sofa inside his living room. It's a time capsule, unchanged after all these years. Paisley-patterned walls, the ancient Zenith TV flanked by a DVD-VHS combo, and in the corner, his military and arm wrestling pins, medals, and trophies on that brass-and-glass shelf, all exactly the same. Even the old khaki La-Z-Boy —the man's throne—hasn't moved from its corner near the brick fireplace.

"You're up," Carter says, standing in the hallway wearing a robe and fuzzy bunny slippers. "Can I get you anything?"

"Water, and anything edible, a cracker if you got it."

"Sure. Give me a second." He moves past the living room and into the kitchen. I hear him opening cupboards, then the fridge, then the sound of liquid pouring. He returns with a glass of water and a Charleston Chew. I take a gulp, then a bite, swallow, and repeat, hoping that the candy will get my mind moving with a sugar rush. Fuck, I can't think straight, and to be perfectly honest, I can't remember how I got here in the first place.

Carter lazily rests on the man's throne and asks, "So ... what's up, dude?"

"What's up?"

"Yeah, what brings you here?"

Through the fog in my head emerges memories of flashing lights and squad cars chasing me at reckless speeds. Gunshots ... explosions.

"They chased me," I mumble, massaging my temples.

"Who chased you?"

"Deputies. In squad cars."

His eyes shift toward a window. The blinds are half closed, and it's dark outside. "Did they follow you here?"

"Nobody followed me ... I lost them miles ago on the Interstate."

Carter returns his gaze to me. "Why were deputies chasing you in the first place?"

It's coming back to me. "I was downtown, you know ... I needed a fix."

"Dude, I told you not to go there."

"I know. I shouldn't have, but I couldn't take it, I was—"

Timothy's bloated face pops into my mind. His huge lips twist into a broken smile as his dead eyes stare at me, then his eyeballs blaze and transform into the headlights of a car. My breath becomes erratic. I'm going to be fucking sick.

"Hey." Carter's voice steadies me. "Are you gonna tell me now what's up with the suit?"

He doesn't know.

"Right," I tell him. More details bubble up, but there's something nipping at me, something more important that I'm not remembering. "The suit. Well, I got arrested and they forced me to work at a mortuary ... this place called J & J Funeral. The owner Jim, he had me moving corpses around town and hauling them back to his warehouse, hence the getup, so—"

"Hold the phone. *You* have been moving dead people?"

"I had to. It was either that or getting my throat cut in jail."

A sharp pain in the inside of my suit bites at me. I shove my hand down my pant leg, yank out the folder I stuffed down there, and toss it on the sofa.

"What the hell is that?" Carter snatches the folder and reads out loud, "Phase Zero Protocols. Where the hell did you get this?"

"I stole it from my boss at the mortuary, Jim."

"Christ, you *stole* it? Then you ran from the law? Who's this person in my living room? Your name *is* Max, isn't it?"

"I'm pretty sure it is."

We riffle through the folder and find that it's filled with new hire forms, celebration of life pamphlets, old gas receipts, and such.

"It's a bunch of crap," Carter says, flipping through page after page. "None of this has anything to do with Phase Zero."

He's right, it's all junk except one piece. There's a handwritten message on a yellow Post-It note.

"Hey, this is kinda weird."

"What do you got?"

"It's from Holtz."

"Well, spit it out. We don't have all day."

I clear my throat then read it out loud. "J & J. We need all of it, plus the trimmings. Holtz."

Carter blinks. "Holtz? As in coffee tycoon Holtz?"

"I assume as in the Governor. She created Phase Zero, right?"

"All of it, plus the trimmings. Huh. What do you think that means?"

"I'm not sure."

Carter loses interest. I set the note beside the

other papers. *Plus the trimmings.* What's that about?

Carter scoots toward me conspiratorially and whispers, "So ... how was it?"

"How was what?"

"Moving bodies ... I've never seen a real dead guy before."

I'm surprised by his comment. I would have thought for sure he would have seen at least *one* corpse in his lifetime. Didn't his mom die?

"Moving bodies?" I lower my voice. "It was ... hard. It's thankless filthy work and yet I suppose ... it's ... necessary." Something keeps nagging at me. Wait, Carter's mom is still alive, just divorced and living her best life somewhere sunny last he mentioned her. But he must have been to his aunt and uncle's funeral when they died of mercury poisoning ...

"Necessary, that's it, huh? Okay Max, or whoever the hell you are." Carter sounds impressed.

Somewhere sunny ... his aunt and uncle ... his cousin ...

"SUNSHINE!" I shout.

"Sunshine what?"

"Her barn—"

"Pops!" Carter interrupts me. "What are you doing out of bed?"

I look over and there's Chuck. He looks half

asleep. Damn, he's lost weight, and his face is as unshaven as his yard. He shuffles toward us and sticks out his hand at me. "I thought I heard a familiar voice. Max, put it there."

I stand to greet him. When we shake, I don't feel the strength of the man I used to know.

"Mr. Jackson, it's so nice to see you. It's been too long."

"Call me Chuck, remember?"

"Of course, Chuck."

"Well, what are you boys up to?" Chuck asks.

"Nothing Pops, you just sit and relax," Carter says. "Let me get your medicine for you." He gets up and as he brushes past me, he ducks his head close to my ear and whispers, "Not a word about what's happened. He can't take the stress right now, doctor's orders." He walks into the kitchen and returns with a glass of water and a handful of pills.

Chuck swallows his pills then says, "Doc says I need these damn things to keep me around longer. I keep telling him they make me feel like crap, but he doesn't seem to care too much about what *I* think."

"Pops, don't be like that," Carter says, frowning. "You won't have to take them forever. Hopefully not much longer."

Chuck looks at me, then lets out a sigh and says, "I was born with some faulty parts, Max.

What are you gonna do? You play the cards you're dealt, right?"

"C'mon Pops, let's get you back to your room. You'll have plenty of time to catch up with Max later, but you look like you still need to rest."

As Carter leads him from the room, Chuck pauses to tell me, "I like the hazmat suit, Max. Looks good on you."

"Thanks Chuck. You take care of yourself."

When they're gone, I grab the documents off the sofa for a second look, and the Post-It note flutters to the floor and lands upside down. Something is attached to its back. What the hell? I snatch it up and fuck me, it's a micro SD card. As I'm examining it closely, I catch an eyeful of cherries-and-berries flashing outside—squad cars!

Deputies storm toward the front door with their guns drawn. I look down at the SD card in my hand.

Hide it!—a voice cries in my head.

They pound at the front door, screaming, "Sheriff's department!"

I stick my tongue out and swallow the card as if it were a tab of acid, a second before two deputies barrel inside. I recognize one—fucking Deputy Asshole again. I make a break toward the kitchen, but I'm too slow. I'm apprehended, frisked, and cuffed. The deputies keep me detained with pistols drawn to my face as they gather the scattered documents.

A towering shadow casts through the front door, followed by heavy steps, and Sheriff Evans walks in with his stupid cowboy hat and an ear-to-ear grin on his face. "Max, what did I say?" he barks. "You mess around, and you'll get my size sixteen boot up your ass. You dumb shit, you just made my day."

21. Size of a golf ball

I fume in the back of Evans's squad car, watching its flashing lights flicker upon Carter's face as he seems to be having a nice old friendly chat with the Sheriff on the front porch. I stare at Carter but he's avoiding eye contact, his chin lowered submissively as Evans tells him something. My *friend* goes back into the house and shuts the front door without acknowledging me. To make matters worse, Deputy Asshole then drives off with my Beast to who-the-fuck-knows-where.

"Max, look at you." Evans slides in and adjusts his rearview mirror. "You look like someone shat a turd down your throat. Hell boy, you're a hundred times worse off than the last time I cuffed you."

I shake my head, too broken to talk. Evans continues, "You have some serious shit stuck to your shoe, Max. Theft, for one. Resisting arrest is two. Property destruction is three. Not to mention you've violated the terms of your work release. You better wash up because you got a hot date with my boot."

I slump into the plastic seat. This can't be happening. I should have stayed in Glacier. Hell, I should have hit the snooze on my alarm and never gotten out of bed the day this all started.

"I have two deputies in the ICU on account of your dumb ass. It's gonna be my personal mission to ensure you never see the light of day again. You hear me, scumbag?"

I stay silent, which digs under Evans's skin. Frustrated, he slams his foot on the gas pedal, sending me flying into the back of the seat. Then he guns it around a roundabout and loses control, fishtailing and driving over the curb, throwing me to the side. My shoulder collides with the rear passenger door and I snap, crying out, "You tubby two-bit moron! You're gonna get us—"

"Shut your trap," he barks at me. I can tell he's pleased he got a reaction out of me. The squad car regains traction, with all four tires now back on the road. "Any more words out of you and I'll stick you in the trunk. Just sit back and try to enjoy the view because you'll never see beyond a cement cell ever again."

A fire builds inside me, fueled by betrayal and

loss. Did Carter fucking sell me out? The thought of being double crossed burns sourly, and I wish I could break out of here and demand a fucking explanation from my so-called friend. Fuck—I'm so ticked I could climb a damn building and scream at the top of my lungs like King-fucking-Kong!

The squad car stops and Sheriff Evans yanks the key from the ignition, then twists toward me. I fixate on his thick eyebrows. They're squished together into a unibrow, and all I want to do is rip that caterpillar off his face and shove it down his double-chin-covered throat.

"Don't you move a damn muscle while I'm gone," Evans tells me, then gets out and walks away.

I disobey his orders and move many muscles, pressing my face against the window glass for a better look. I watch Evans hoofing it toward a large two-story brick building. The sun is long gone, and I can't make out many details. Most of the windows of the building are dark except on the second story, where a few radiate blue light. It seems that we're parked atop a hill. I can see Mount Baker in the distance, and a cluster of trailers below. It looks like Oak—

ZOOM!

A bicycle races past my window, inches from the glass, then two more. They circle the squad car like NASCAR drivers, going around and around until they're a single blur of orange and chrome. They stop, and the three cyclists kickstand their worn-out Schwinn cruisers. It's those ginger thieves again.

The tallest of the bunch is staring at me, licking his lips like he hasn't eaten in months, his tongue brushing over his peach-fuzz 'stache. He snaps his pale fingers, and like a rehearsed act in a play, the gingers have me surrounded. The tallest is against my rear window, another to my left, and the smallest one's at the front. The little guy pounds his fists against the squad car's hood, and I jump back against my seat, startled. All three giggle, which escalates until they're cackling like hyenas.

"Shut up!" I yell, but my demands make them more animalistic. They pound on the squad car with their feet and fists, snorting, slobbering all over the aluminum and glass. They're filthy. With their ratty orange hair and torn clothes, they look as if they live in a hole underground.

"What the fuck do you guys want?" I ask.

The tallest taps the rear window glass with his knuckles then makes a thumbs-up sign, grinning. I show him an identical gesture with my cuffed hands behind my back and ask, "Are we cool or what?"

He says nothing and stares at me like a dead-eyed shark, his grin vanishing. His freckled thumb raises toward his Adam's apple then motions across his throat. The bastard's just messing with me. He erupts into another laughing fit while the younger two start rocking the squad car back and forth. The suspension squeaks and the CB radio attached to the dash jolts loose, tumbling down. The smallest ginger climbs up the hood to the roof and bounces on it as if the car were a giant trampoline.

BANG!

A gunshot rings out and the little one drops from the roof to the pavement.

Sheriff Evans yells, "What did I tell you, three? You carrot-top bike-pedalin' sons-of-bitches! Don't fuck with my ride!"

The remaining two run to their bikes and pedal away, leaving the youngest behind. I peer out the side window and see that the kid has a hole in his head the size of a golf ball. His blood and brains are oozing out into the parking lot, and I watch the last of his nerves twitch until they don't. He's dead.

Evans is a goddamn maniac.

The car's trunk opens and through a gap, I see Sheriff Evans. Standing next to him is a quivering and cuffed man, shirtless and gagged. Across his belly is Sharpied a large circle, followed by a short horizontal line. Evans forces the guy into the trunk and slams the lid shut. The man flails and kicks, vibrating my seat. This is one fucked-up massage chair.

Evans whistles the tune of "Yankee Doodle" as he nonchalantly steps over the boy he shot and plants his ass in his seat. He reattaches the fallen radio and stops whistling. It's quiet, except for the man in the trunk thrashing behind me.

Evans makes a call, holding his cell phone close to his ear. "Yeah, we have a fresh one at the school. Nah. Nothing like that, sixty, seventy pounds tops. See you then." Click. He adjusts his rearview mirror until he can see me straight in the eyes and says, "You know Max, there's two kinds of people in this world. You're either essential, or you're stuck in the trunk."

He laughs to himself while he fires up the engine. "Stuck in the trunk!" he repeats between breaths, seeming to find his choice of words extremely hilarious. We take off with his cherries-and-berries crackling into the evening sky.

The Sheriff flips on the radio to a classical channel and an orchestra begins to play, Bach maybe. Evans twists the volume knob up, then shouts, "I love this classic! It's so mighty, like me!" He waves his arm in the air as if conducting the orchestra.

Evans is utterly insane. Fuck this, I've got to get the hell away from him.

My heart is racing and I'm about to lose it for real-real. I close my eyes and take a humongous breath. Trying to calm myself, I imagine a world without Evans, without Jim, or Junior, or Noah. A world without Phase Zero, without a lockdown, without HIT.

I can't do it. All I see is Evans's ugly fucking face laughing at me. My hopeful fantasy is overtaken by ghoulish visions of military jets shooting down Zeppelins and passenger planes. Bombs blowing up bridges and destroying peaceful cities. Phase Zero signs on closed businesses, millions of people losing their homes, losing their sanity as chaos floods the streets with bullets, fires, and panic that spreads throughout the world.

I can't calm down.

Images of war machines driving through homes, humans hog-tied and pistol-whipped, people murdering one another over water, over a loaf of bread. Blood flowing into the streets.

Breathe, Max.

I watch the last polar bear on Earth collapse from starvation and get picked clean by vultures. I see my own face, and a giant tear runs down my cheek. The drop falls to the soil and my mother sprouts up as if from a seed, and she says, *Fly.* She morphs into Sunshine, and she's perched on the roof of her burning barn like a gargoyle, surrounded by rising flames. I climb up the barn's siding, but I lose my grip and fall, fall, fall into a deep, dark cement cell with no way out. I beat the concrete with my fists until my knuckles become dust, screaming "I want a do-over!" until my vocal cords tear.

The cement walls shrink, closing in on me and crushing me. I'm reincarnated into a moth on a dandelion in a desolate field. I feel the Earth's temperature rising, the ozone thinning. I watch our sun swell into a red giant, engulfing our entire planet. Everything we once loved becomes stardust, scattered into empty space.

The squad car screeches to a halt.

"Up and at 'em, we're here," Evans hollers, rolling out from his seat. *Here* is unknown. All I can make out is that it's pitch dark with a hint of vinegary odor. Evans grabs my shoulder and tosses me to the cement floor.

"You dick," I spit.

Evans bends down and slaps me across my face. I taste blood pooling in my mouth. "What did I tell you about saying another word, dipshit?" Evans points his hairy index finger at his boot. "Now shut the hell up." He pulls me to my feet by my handcuffs. "Stay here," he tells me, then taps his holstered .38. He moves to the trunk of his car and raps his fists against the lid in a playful pattern as if he were a friend knocking at your door. "Yoo-hoo," he says. "If you'll be a good boy, I'll let you out."

A muffled groan responds, and Evans asks, "What's that? Santa can't hear you." He shakes his keys to the beat of "Jingle Bells."

"Ho ho ho," Evans sings out, shaking the keys like a maraca. He releases the trunk latch, pulls out the bound man, then slams the trunk shut. He loses his playful manner. "Move, you two," he barks. "And don't make me tell you twice."

It's so incredibly dark I can't see the floor beneath my feet, and it feels like I could walk off the edge of a cliff at any moment. Where is he taking us?

"Stop!" Evans yells, yanking my cuffed wrists so hard my head whiplashes.

I hear an electric *POP!* A brilliant light floods the room, momentarily blinding me. I can't see shit, but my ears pick up a bone-chilling voice from nearby.

"Maxwell. Boy oh boy, have we missed you."

22. WHATEVER PASSING THOUGHT

My pupils shrink, adjusting to the sudden light. I'm back in the J & J warehouse; that explains the smell. I see Jim a few paces in front of me, gripping the PHASE ZERO PROTOCOLS folder in his hands. Flanking him are his minions, Noah and Junior.

The minions' eyes are black saucers, and Junior still has a blood-stained apron wrapped around his torso, which pulsates as he breathes heavily, nearly panting. Jim's lips curl into a smile and he says to them, "Looks like you two are gonna be busy this afternoon."

Sheriff Evans wraps his sweaty hand around my trembling forearm and tugs firmly, reminding me I'm in no position to fuck around; I'm under their control. I scan my newly visible surroundings. Beyond the three J & J stooges toward the back of the warehouse, I see a glowing exit sign and parked below it, my Beast. Her boxy rear end is flung open, and two empty gurneys lie unfolded beside her.

Jim hands the folder to Noah then walks toward me. His heels clang on the cement like the hooves of a Clydesdale prancing down a cobblestone street. Evans shoves me forward and I stumble, but before I eat shit on the cement floor, Jim catches me.

"Hey Maxie-poo, I got you," Jim croons, setting me to my feet. His breath stinks of rotten fish and mint chewing gum. He brushes off my shoulders like a maid dusting a lampshade. "Let me have a look at ya," he says as he circles me. "You're not looking so hot these days."

Jim pinches my hip and I squirm. "Oh Maxwell, have you lost weight? Well, you're in luck. Do you see Junior over there? He's an expert at *fixing* people, if you know what I mean."

He continues to walk around me. "Maxwell ... I know where you've been. I know what you've done. I know what you've seen, and now you're going to pay ... Sheriff. What do we do with thieves during Phase Zero?"

"Ha!" Evans laughs. "The penalty is capital punishment."

Jim looks at me squarely and says, "Theft is a serious crime indeed."

My mouth unhinges. "Jim, listen, I—"

"Maxwell. Do us both a favor and let whatever passing thought of an excuse is in your thick head fade into the sunset because you ain't talking your way out of this shit." Then, like a striking rattlesnake, Jim grabs me by the collar of my suit and says, "Who do you think you're messing with? I've got fucking eyes in the back of my head!"

Jim releases me and strokes the five o'clock stubble on his chin before continuing. "I was about to make you one of us ... essential ... but then you had to fuck it all up, and that kind of behavior is a no-no that I can't let you get away with. I'm going to start by penalizing your entire bloodline."

"What?"

"Shut up!" Jim backhands me. "When people take from me, I take from them ten times. Tell you what Maxwell, since I'm in a jolly mood, I'll let you say your last goodbyes to her remains. I mean, this is a funeral home after all." Jim saunters over to Junior and runs his finger through the sticky mess on the apron he's wearing. "You see this? This is your mother." Jim holds up his bloody finger and licks it clean. "She tastes sweet, Maxwell, liquid gold sweetness."

My head feels detached from my body. I'm weightless and numb, like I'm about to faint. I mumble, "No ... You're not gonna—"

Before I can finish my sentence, Jim's hand

grips my throat, crushing my esophagus. "I said shut up," he snaps. I choke and cough, unable to breathe. "Your mother was remarkable, Maxwell. A perfect match. Christ, we must have pumped out five or six quarts from her. She was a big payday for us around here. Junior was able to scrape some high-dollar parts from her as well, ain't that right, Junior?"

I can't turn my head, but I hear no-neck Junior panting like a trained dog in response.

Jim pats my stomach with his free hand. "How does that old saying go? Like mother, like son? You're also full of high-dollar goods inside that skinny belly of yours. You and your mother are going to make us rich, son. Maxwell, I've been meaning to ask you, can I call you son?"

If his hand weren't still clenched around my throat, I would answer by spitting in his face.

Jim shifts his weight to one side, head crooked. "Too flattered to answer? Hell, I'm gonna assume it's alright with you then, *son*. I like the sound of that. So, son, here's what's gonna happen from here on out. Noah will strap you and your shirtless companion on one of my lovely gurneys, then Junior will do what Junior does best. What do you think about that, son?"

Fuck Jim. Fuck Junior, fuck Noah, fuck Evans, fuck all of you. I'm out of here on the count of ten. *Ten.*

Jim continues. "Don't answer because I know precisely what you're thinking in that worthless brain of yours. Jim, sir, boss-man, daddy, what is it that Junior does best? Well son, to put it matter-of-factly, Junior will extract every bit of your precious blood from your pathetic little body until he can't squeeze another drop."

Nine.

"Then, well, I'd hate to spoil the surprise for you, but fuck it, I'll give it to you straight."

Eight.

"He's gonna rip out your essentials, starting with your fucking liver, well, eighty percent of it, leaving a little behind so you can regenerate a new one. We're gonna keep you teetering on the edge of death, and then repeat this painful process of cutting and regrowing until you fucking croak. Can you believe that? Son, you're like a goddamn goose that lays golden eggs." Jim kisses my forehead.

Seven. Six.

Jim releases me and steps to the side, allowing Noah and Junior a clear path to me. "Now son, I'm gonna release you to these fine body movers, but before I do, I'll give you a choice. Do you wanna go under the knife first or second?"

Five.

I growl, my throat raw and aching, "You'll

never get away with this, you know that? My friends are gonna be coming for me."

"Friends? Are you talking about your so-called friend Carter? Son, I'm a hundred steps ahead of you. Your boy Carter is part of this. He and I have an agreement that I doubt he would sabotage for the likes of *you*. Or do you mean your pretty little girlfriend Sunshine? Don't you know she works for me now?"

Four. Three.

I shake my head. "No, she would never work for the likes of you."

"Son, I'm sorry if the truth hurts. If I had known you were all hot and heavy for that one, I would have—well, it doesn't matter anymore, does it?"

Two.

"You're gonna pay for this Jim, you stupid bastard."

"Stupid? Son, you're the one who's not so clever, because if you were, you would have thought that *maybe* my meat wagon was trackable. My girl Samantha gave me the exact coordinates to where you were at all times. Oh boy, I thought you kids with your computers and handheld horseshit were supposed to be smart?"

Samantha, you double-crossing bitch.

"Would you look at the time," Jim says, peering at his bare wrist. "It's your bedtime, son."

Jim snaps his fingers. "Junior. Noah. Get these idiots out of here, pronto!"

One.

Noah and Junior shuffle toward the gurneys, and a voice inside my head screams *RUN!* Time slows as I take off toward the exit at the far end of the warehouse. My muscles tense and sounds become distorted like I've inhaled a balloon full of nitrous.

"Geeeeetttt hhhhiiiiiiimmmm!" Jim screams.

I'm near the exit, and I might make it. I can almost taste the cool air of freedom beyond the walls of this fucked funeral home. Then, I'm smashed from behind by what feels like a dump truck.

Zero.

23. Sea of terror

"Mmmmfgggghhh! Nnnnmmmmfffff!"

I regain consciousness to the muffled sounds of agony and horror behind me. I try to sit up but find that I'm tied down to a gurney, and I've been stripped down to my briefs. A pencil-sized chrome syringe is stuck in my left arm, and it hurts like a hornet sting. The needle is attached to a tube that feeds a blood-filled bag hooked on a metal pole. I see an upside-down mark Sharpied on my bare chest. Like the mark on the guy in the trunk, it's a circle followed by a dash. O- ... my blood type.

"Nggggffrrrrrrgbbb!"

I look around and see the corrugated metal walls of a shipping container. It's brightly lit with fluorescent shop lights and stinks with that familiar sharp smell, like pickles. To my right is a floor-to-ceiling shelf crowded with jars. They're filled with what looks like flesh-colored vegetables suspended in clear goo. I squint—the labels slapped on the jars read: SPLEEN, KIDNEY, LIVER, HEART—*fuck!* I shudder involuntarily.

"Rrffbbbggmrrr!"

I tug on my restraints, but they're tight and don't give an inch. Severe nausea rushes through me as my mother's words repeat in my head.

Everyone will end up six feet underground. There's nothing you can do.

My mother's blood on Junior's apron. They fucking killed her. I'm dizzy, close to passing out from panic and blood loss, but now is not the time for a nap, Max. *Breathe, Max.*

Just when I think it can't get worse, a menacing electric buzz engulfs the room. The buzzing grows louder as if it's met resistance and needs to work harder. Specks of blood spatter across the walls.

Bzzzzzz! Bzzzzzzzzzzzzzzz!

I want to close my ears, to shut out the horror of it all, but I can't. The sound is all-consuming, surrounding me, drowning me in a sea of terror.

Bzzzzzzzzzzzzzzzzz!

I feel myself teetering on the cliff's edge of insanity. I take one giant breath, then a second, then a third, but the gulps of air only make me start to hyperventilate.

Bzzzzzzzzzzzzzzz!

Somehow in the midst of my freakout, I muster up enough strength to scream at the top of my lungs, "LET ME GO YOU BASTARD!"

The buzzing ceases and Junior's face appears inches above mine, upside down and blocking the overhead light like a moon eclipsing the sun. His head is soaked with blood. Warm drops drip onto my face; I shake myself like a wet dog, but the sticky liquid clings to me like a second skin. Junior's dead black eyes bore into mine, and I feel the dark force of his gaze. I know without a doubt that I'm in the company of a psychopath.

Junior's lips move. He can talk?

"I'm afraid that's not possible. You see, Max, you are not merely an incidental participant; you are an indispensable element intricately woven into the fabric of this grand experiment. Not to mention, releasing you would surely disrupt the delicate balance we strive to achieve here, impeding our progress toward wealth and power beyond what your feeble mind could comprehend."

"Junior, you—you don't have to do this," I stutter. "Just let me go and I'll be on my way." My begging falls on deaf ears, and Junior simply shakes his head. There is no plea deal with this guy. I'm at his mercy.

Junior withdraws from my sight, and the buzzing begins anew.

Bzzz—

Miraculously the buzzing stops, followed by an orchestra of smacks and grunts from behind me. I hear a thump like a heavy sack of flour dropping to the floor.

"Max! Are you okay?"

"Carter?" I ask, my voice ragged. Carter's head pops into view from above, followed by Chuck's. Chuck's suited up in camo gear with gobs of army-green paint smeared across his freshly clean-shaven cheeks.

Carter wastes no time using a box cutter to free me from my restraints. I force myself upright and turn to see what's behind me. The remains of the man from the trunk, sternum sawed into pieces, lie strapped to another gurney. Chunks of his flesh and puddles of blood are all over the floor. Below him, Junior is slumped against the legs of the gurney next to a blood-soaked Sawzall. I turn away from the hideous sight.

"Is he dead?"

"Which one?" Carter asks.

"Fuck off, the one with the Sawzall, obviously."

"Nope." Carter waves a soggy white rag in his hand. "Works like a charm."

Chuck pulls the hollow needle from my arm,

and my DNA squirts all over the room. "Give it pressure and it'll be fine," he tells me.

Carter tears off a chunk of duct tape from a roll and wraps it around my wound, saying, "That should hold for a while." Carter stuffs his rag, box cutter, and tape into his backpack and slings it over his shoulder.

As glad as I am to see them, my mind is seething. I get right to it and say, "Carter, you got something you wanna tell me?"

"What the hell are you talking about?" he asks.

"Jim. Did you make some kind of deal with him?" I glare at him.

"No," Carter says, scowling. He meets my eyes. "I don't know what you're talking about."

"My old boss, the funeral home director, Jim. The prick who threw me in here. He said he has some kind of agreement with you."

"I didn't agree to anything." Carter pauses, purses his lips, then continues. "There was something I was going to tell you. Some asshole called me today before you showed up. He said that he has a matching liver for Pops. He knew all about his condition, his blood type, weight, everything. It was creepy. He said he could arrange an operation, but that there was a catch. The catch being, I had to let him know if you, Maxwell Maddison, were to try to get a hold of me. I told him to go fuck himself. *Obviously*."

"Why didn't you tell me?"

"Well, you showed up with the hazmat suit and your beefed-up Beast and your insane stories, running from the law, moving dead people, what the shit? Dude, it was as if you were someone else. I was going to mention that call, but seeing you like that got me caught up in the moment. I promise on my fucking life, I had nothing to do with the pigs showing up. I would never rat you out. As soon as the pigs left, Pops made me tell him what the hell is going on, then he jumped out of bed and insisted we come find you and break you free."

"It's true, Max," Chuck confirms.

"I haven't seen him this full of life in months!" Carter exclaims. "We did some recon at the precinct and overheard talk about J & J, and then I remembered you telling me about the warehouse out back, so we raced over."

I deeply exhale, tension leaving my shoulders. "I believe you, Carter, it's fine. And uh, thanks for saving my ass again."

"Anytime, brother."

"Say, Max," Chuck says. "How do you suppose the Sheriff knew you were at my place?"

"An AI did me in."

"AI?"

"Yep. That fucker Jim installed artificial intelligence software inside the Beast called Samantha."

"So, this Samantha thing tracked you?" Chuck asks.

"Yeah, she ratted me out." Noah's words echo inside my head: *She knows everything about everyone.* "And fuck, she has access to the state's medical databases."

"So that's how Jim knew about my medical condition?" Chuck asks.

"Yeah, I think so Chuck. She knows everyone ... including my mother ... fuck ... my mother."

"What's up with your mom?" Carter asks.

"They killed her, man—Jim. Evans. We gotta get those bastards!" I try getting to my feet, but my knees are as wobbly as a newborn fawn's.

"Take it easy, Max. You lost a lot of blood." Carter hands me a Charleston Chew. "Eat this, man. You need your strength."

I take his advice and take a big bite of the sugary treat. It's delicious. Carter and Chuck snoop around as I keep chewing.

"Jesus, look at this place," Chuck says, looking at the wall of human organs.

"This is batshit crazy!" Carter exclaims.

"This Jim is one sick fuck," Chuck says, raising a jar close to his face. "I haven't seen anything like this since '74."

I finish eating the chocolate and feel a hell of a lot better. I try to stand again, and after a few shaky steps, I can maintain my balance. I look around for my clothes, but all I can find are my boots in the corner. I lace them on tight, then join Carter and Chuck standing next to the remains of the man from the trunk. The guy looks even worse close up, as if a grizzly's chewed him to pieces. His rib cage has been hollowed out, and his guts are piled in a five-gallon bucket beside the gurney labeled ESSENTIALS.

Carter asks me, "Did you know him?"

"Before today, I'd never seen him," I tell him. "Poor guy."

"Hey, what's this?" Chuck asks. Chuck has Junior's head twisted to one side in his hands. On the back of his neck is a finger-length scar. I kneel down next to Chuck and see old stitches of black thread criss-crossing the scar.

"What the devil is that about?" Chuck asks as he drops Junior's skull, which bounces on the ground. He's out cold, his eyes closed, and I'm glad—I couldn't take more of that evil stare.

"I'm not sure, Chuck."

"Max, isn't this Sunshine's?"

Carter is holding up a clear glass vial with a yellow smiley face sticker on it.

"Fuck, they have her working—"

"Who's they?" Carter asks.

"Jim. He said he has Sunshine."

"What? Where?" Chuck and Carter ask simultaneously.

Like lightning, an image flashes in my mind—the blue glow in the windows I saw from the back of the Sheriff's car.

"The fucking Falls, that's where."

24. I'LL SCALP THESE DICKWEEDS

We abandon the gruesome scene in the shipping container, leaving the mutilated man and Junior, and navigate through the warehouse toward the exit. The lights are on but it's eerily deserted—no sign of Jim, Noah, Evans, or my Beast anywhere.

Outside, we're greeted by dark skies and thick mist. I can feel a heavy pressure in the air. Snow's coming. Freezing wind brushes against my bare calves. Fuck, it's cold. My nipples are hard as rocks and I don't complain; my comfort's the last thing I give a shit about right now. I just want to leave this fucked-up place and find Sunshine before it's too late.

"What are you guys driving?" I ask.

"My safari wagon," Chuck replies.

I follow Carter and Chuck past the employee

parking lot and down a grassy hill. We continue, passing evergreens and gravestones, then hidden behind a low-hanging tree bough is Chuck's Jeep. It's an older forest-green Wrangler with the soft top peeled back. Chuck takes the wheel, Carter jumps in next to him, and I climb into the rear. Carter tosses me a wool blanket and I wrap it around myself.

The Jeep lurches forward, its tires gripping the loose soil as we speed, hurling down a narrow backwoods trail better suited for hikers. The suspension bounces wildly until we make contact with a paved road. Chuck stays clear of the major streets, driving through back alleys and bike paths. Sounds of emergency sirens wail in the not-so-distance.

Along the way, I tell them about seeing Sunshine's blue lights at the school in Oak Falls, about how Jim tracked her down through her fingerprints on the vial, and about the fire. I feel like a piece of crap—if I hadn't tried to get a fix and gotten arrested, they wouldn't have found her vial in the first place.

We pass the Lettered Streets near downtown, and I catch glimpses of people peeking through the windows of their homes, looking scared shitless like caged cattle in a slaughterhouse moments before being turned into ground beef. Phase Zero has consumed our town, shattering its spirit and dreams. Please don't tell me this is the new normal.

We sneak out of Bellingham and somehow make it unhindered to the outskirts of the Falls. However, now the sky is filled with snow flurries, and it's getting harder to see. Chuck slows the Jeep to a crawl, dodging overthrown trash bins and junked cars. He pulls over to a curb. "Where to, boys?"

"The school should be on top of a hill around here somewhere," I tell him. "But I can't see a damn thing."

Chuck reaches under his seat and withdraws a pair of high-tech binoculars. He wipes off its lenses with his camo sleeve and hands it to me, saying, "This should help. They've got night vision."

I raise the binoculars to my eyes, and the world through the lenses glows bright green. I pan around us and luckily, the flurries settle for a moment. "There. Up ahead and to the right. The school has two stories, brick walls."

"I *think* I see it," Carter says unconfidently.

I keep looking through my green filter. Flurries scatter from a gust, revealing a few Chevy vans parked beside the school with the J & J logo. "Meat wagons," I say grimly.

"What?" Carter asks.

"Chevy vans, they belong to J & J."

A swarm of deputies march into my zoomed-in view and begin pulling shrink-wrapped bodies from the meat wagons. A moment later, a black SUV pulls in front of the vans, the words "Meat Wagon #4" on its side. A familiar figure steps down from the driver's seat. "It's Jim," I growl. "He's up there, and he's driving my Beast!"

"Well, what are we waiting for? Let's get him!" Carter yells, excited.

"Hold up," I tell him. "He's got dozens of deputies with him."

"So we can't just blast through the doors," Chuck says calmly, the voice of reason. "We need to creep up from behind. A surprise attack is our best plan."

"He's right," I agree. "We need to find a back way in."

Chuck drives toward the school. The road worsens and the Jeep jolts and bounces, the suspension groaning under the strain. I can't stop thinking about the Beast. I miss her; it's been too long without her.

The brakes lock up and Chuck shouts, "Hey! Get off the road."

Two hooded kids on bikes are jamming the route. Chuck lays down the horn, but they don't seem fazed. They kickstand their two-wheelers and walk toward us.

"What's their problem?" Chuck asks.

"Don't know. All I know is that we don't have time for this shit," Carter says.

Chuck attempts to drive around them but they dance with the Jeep, staying in front of its grill. They're close enough now that I can see orange hairs sticking out from the sides of their hoods, lit up like halos by the Jeep's headlights. Oh great, these assholes again.

Carter leans forward and squints. "I know these fucks, Max. Those shits stole our toilet paper! Just run 'em over, Pops."

"Calm down, son," Chuck says. "It's just a couple of kids messing with us, is all."

"Calm down? They fucking maced—"

"Hold up." I put my hand on Carter's shoulder. "We're on their turf. Maybe they can help."

"Are you serious, Max? Them? Help us?"

"They might know a way inside the school. Carter, do you have a picture of Sunshine on your phone?"

"Yeah, of course."

"Give it to me. I'm gonna have a chat with them. Chuck, keep the engine running."

I hop out of the Jeep and approach the kids with one hand holding up my blanket-cloak and the other holding out Sunshine's digital photo. I call out, "Listen up, we don't want any trouble, we just want to talk. We're looking for this woman."

I must look like an insane person, wild-eyed

with a blanket wrapped around my torso, my skinny legs poking out into boots. But it's the Falls and they must be used to a high level of insanity because they stand still and allow me to approach.

"Her name is Sunshine, and we think she's being held hostage inside that school." I point up the hill. "Have you seen her?"

The taller ginger glances at her photo then says, "Maybe." His voice squeaks as if his balls haven't dropped yet. He's younger than I thought, despite his height and wispy peach fuzz.

"Do you know a back way into the school? A way we can get in undetected?"

"Maybe."

"Can you take us there?"

"Maybe."

The smaller kid pipes up. "What's in it for us?"

I lower my chin and stare straight at them. "Sweet revenge."

They glance at one another, then the taller one repeats, "Revenge?"

"You help us inside the school, help us find her, and I'll give you the Sheriff's head on a platter. That fucker murdered your brother, right? Help us get inside, and we'll give you the revenge that you deserve. That, I fucking promise."

They huddle together for a moment, whispering. Then the taller ginger looks at me. "Deal," he says. "We know a secret way in."

"Great," I say with a sigh of relief. "What's your names?"

He says, "Quinn. And this is my little brother, Simon."

"Hi Quinn, Simon. I'm Max, and the guy driving the Jeep is Chuck. Sunshine's his niece. And the other guy's his son, my best friend Carter."

Quinn sheds a thin smile and says, "I remember him. Follow us."

I climb back inside the Jeep and say, "They're gonna get us into the school, so follow them."

"What the fuck? Why?" Carter sputters. "What did you say to them? What are you, the ginger whisperer now?"

I explain what happened with the Sheriff and their brother, and my promise of revenge. Carter mutters *fuck* to himself, but agrees we can trust them for the time being.

The Jeep struggles to keep up with the kids' Schwinns through narrow and twisting roads. Quinn and Simon take a sharp right down a trail that descends steeply into a thick, snow-frosted forest.

"What the fuck is this? Looks to me like a trap," Carter grouches, crossing his arms.

"It's just an old lumber road, son," Chuck says.

"Can your Jeep make it down?" I ask.

"My Jeep can rock and roll down any road. I'll move her into four-low."

Chuck shifts the Jeep into gear. Tree limbs smack against the Jeep's frame, shaking loose clumps of snow into the cab, and stones kick up underneath. It's a treacherous path, yet the kids don't seem fazed; they bomb down the slope and screech to a stop at its base. Chuck parks near them and kills the engine.

Quinn waves for us to get out of our vehicle, so we exit the Jeep and survey our surroundings. Here, the path widens into a clearing with a steep drop-off on one side into a canyon. I walk toward the overlook and in the distance, I can see majestic Mount Baker. The view is breathtaking, and I could sit here and soak it in all day, except I'm not here to sightsee.

But one thing I don't see here is the school.

Was Carter right? Are these gingers fucking with us?

I approach Quinn and demand, "Where's the school?" My heart thumps in my chest as I wait for his response.

"This way," he says. He heads straight into the woods.

Carter whispers to me, "I'll scalp these dickweeds if I have to, Max. Fucking believe it."

We follow the kids, bushwhacking through

snow, frozen mud, and the thorny remnants of last summer's blackberry vines. After a while, Carter asks, "Pops, how you doing back there?"

"This ain't my first time in the jungle, son."

My skin is scratched, my blanket is torn and hardly hanging on, and I'm one hundred percent over being in the woods. Just when I'm about to ask where the hell they're taking us, Quinn says, "Here." He pulls back a broken tree branch, revealing a drainpipe large enough for all of us to walk into.

"I'll be damned," Carter mumbles.

Quinn and Simon walk into the pipe as if walking through the front door of a house. Their footsteps splash as they tread through water, and within seconds, they disappear from view.

Carter pulls out a flashlight from his backpack and flicks it on, aiming the light into the drainpipe. "Are we doing this?" he asks.

I look at Chuck, and there's a sparkle in his eyes. He looks like the Chuck I knew growing up, like he has a few more fights left in him.

"What the hell are we waiting for?" Chuck says. "Come on. Close together now."

Carter steps in first with his flashlight beaming forward, and Chuck follows. I take a deep breath and join them.

25. The shit-eater

We tail Quinn and Simon through the cement drainpipe. The stench inside is unbearable, worse than anything I've ever endured, and I've endured a *lot* of stench in the last couple of days. I'd call myself an expert on the subject, in fact.

It's one hundred percent pure filth in here, not to mention ultrahazardous. Without Carter's trusty flashlight, my head would collide with the tunnel's sides, or I could easily slice my soles on the countless shards of glass sprinkled across the swampy floor. I have no idea how our guides are navigating without a light of their own. What, can gingers see in the dark?

We travel down the pipe for what feels like hours. I hate this and I start thinking that maybe we should turn around, maybe this *is* a trap.

Carter voices what I've been wondering. "Hey you two! How much farther do we have to go down this goddamn shithole?"

Quinn responds confidently with one word: "Close."

Close? Portland is relatively close. *Fucking London is reasonably* close *compared to the distance to the Moon. Close compared to what?*

Suddenly the stench increases tenfold, and now a buzzing like radio static fills my ears.

"Guys, do you hear that?" I ask.

"Sure do," Chuck says. "Sounds like damn locusts."

"Yeah, and it smells like a spoiled compost heap," Carter adds.

"So, it's not just me," I say. "I thought I might be going crazy."

A plump fly lands on my nose. I swat at the shit-eater, miss, and smack my own face. As we trek on, the static grows as loud as a tsunami warning. Suddenly they descend—a goddamn cyclone of relentless flies, what must be thousands of the chubby shit-lovers swirling around us. They try to crawl into my ears, nostrils, mouth, every crevice in my face. I lower my head against the insect storm and tent my blanket around me.

"What's with the flies?" Carter yells.

Chuck replies, "Heck if I know."

We keep walking, shielding ourselves as best

as we can. I'm two seconds from saying *fuck this place, let's take our chances and drive the Jeep right through the school's fucking front door*. But before I can get a single word out, the tunnel opens up to a cavernous space the size of an airplane hangar.

As he scans the chamber with his flashlight, Carter fumbles and drops it into a puddle. Its light blinks out. He fishes it out of the water, but it's fried. "I fucked up," Carter mutters, smacking the handle against his thigh.

A faint light sheds down from above through metal grates in the arched ceiling. It's not much, but once our eyes adjust, we can at least see enough to keep walking.

We see Quinn and Simon ahead standing close to a wall and hurry to catch up to them.

Carter twirls, swatting at the swarm around him. He cries out, "Enough is enough! How do we get inside the fucking school?"

The kids jerk their chins upward. We follow their gazes to see iron steps plugged high into the cement wall, up to a covered utility hole in the ceiling some thirty feet from the ground.

"How are we gonna reach that?" Carter asks.

He has a good point. The bottom step is beyond reach, at least halfway up.

Chuck moves closer to the wall and rubs his chin, examining the distance.

"What do you think, Chuck?" I ask.

"Well, I'm six-two, and you guys are about five-nine and a buck fifty each, and our fearless guides are five-foot-whatever and a hundred pounds soaking wet. If my math is correct and we climb up each other's shoulders, minus the heads, and carry over the torsos, we *might* make it."

"Okay, sure, we *might* make it," Carter says, "but in this scenario you'd be at the bottom, right? What about you, Pops? How would you make it out?"

"Rope," says Simon. He points up.

"There's rope up there?" I ask him. He nods. I turn to Chuck. "Are you positive you can handle us on your shoulders? I'd hate to see you get—"

"Hurt?" Chuck's chest puffs out. "Max, hurt is when you run into enemy territory and step on a booby trap and get your leg blown off. Shit Max, I'm a Marine and a state arm wrestling champion, remember? I might not be in the finest shape, but I'll be damned if I'll let this little obstacle impede bringing my niece—"

"Help! Over here!" Cries from the kids stop Chuck mid-sentence. I hadn't even noticed those sneaky gingers run off. We hustle toward their voices, and when we pinpoint them, we're absolutely dumbfounded. They're standing beside a mound of rotten human flesh, a decaying pile of tangled corpses crawling with maggots and flies, and—*fuck me sideways*—like the guy from the trunk, the bodies have been gutted.

Quinn and Simon drags half of a corpse from the pile past us, each pulling an arm. I look down and it's Timothy's upper torso. He's been split in half. *Fucking hell*. They drop Tim's mutilated remains beneath the steps.

Chuck mumbles "Genius," then plucks an arm from the pile and calls out to us, "We don't have all day. Hop to it, fellas."

Carter and I share a moment, staring at each other and shaking our heads. "Fuck it," he says, shrugging. We work together in a single file, a chain gang passing fly-infested bodies down the line and stacking them below the iron steps. Here I am, I think to myself. Moving bodies again.

The flies furiously buzz our heads as we disturb their dinner. I'm going to puke my guts out all over the place, I just know it, but Carter beats me to it. He leans against the wall, blowing gobs.

I spot a stiff about my size buried in the pile, and I pull him out by his feet. He's wearing navy coveralls with embroidery over the breast that says 'Joseph.' I can't run around in a blanket all day, and Joseph's coveralls don't look too bad. I rip them off and slip on my new threads. It's an okay fit. A little baggy and stained with blood and bile, but hey, beggars can't be choosers, right?

Once we have enough bodies stacked, we

scramble up to the summit of Flesh Mountain and form ourselves into a human totem pole. I'm sitting on Chuck's shoulders and Carter is on mine with Quinn on his. For the cherry on top, Simon climbs to our crest and on tippy-toes, he reaches his freckled hand out for the lowest iron step. I keep my shoulders tense, trying not to squirm. My back feels ready to give out at any second, and Chuck is trembling below me. If he goes down, we're all screwed.

The little guy grips the step with both hands and pulls himself up, his feet dangling as he grabs the next step, then another, until he reaches the top. He pushes the utility hole lid open with his head and climbs through.

Chuck starts to wiggle like a bowl of Jell-O. He yells, "Mayday! I'm going down!" His legs buckle and we all tumble down like Jenga pieces onto the pile of rotting flesh. My foot gets stuck inside some poor chick's rib cage. Carter's face plunges between a corpse's ass cheeks. Quinn somehow lands on his feet like a goddamn cat.

Carter frees himself, throws his head back, and screams.

"Everyone okay?" Chuck asks as he gets back to his feet.

Carter's up and retching again, but he seems to be in one piece. "Are you fucking kidding me?" he yells between heaves.

One end of a thick rope drops from above and dangles beside us. I look up and Simon is peering down at us, smiling.

Carter and Quinn waste no time scurrying up the rope, reaching the top, and pulling themselves through the utility hole. Chuck insists I go next, and I know better than to argue with the guy so with the rope between my legs, I pull myself up, bracing my boots against the wall for added leverage. It's about as fun as I remember from high school gym class, which is to say not at all. Little by little, I make it, and when I'm within an arm's reach, Carter extends his hand down. We clasp wrists and he yanks me up with one big heave-ho.

I collapse on my back, catching my breath on the cement floor. A bare bulb suspended from the ceiling casts its light upon several industrial tanks spaced throughout the small room we're now in.

KA-CHINK-KA-CHUNK!

My attention jumps toward a shaking tank. The legs rattle as one of its valves whistles, spewing steam.

"Where are we?" I ask.

"The boiler room," Carter replies. He walks toward a steel eye bolt sunk in cement where the end of the rope is tied. Tugging on the rope several times to test it, he yells, "Pops! Are you ready?"

"Born ready, son!"

Chuck manhandles the rope, neck muscles

flexing as he pulls himself off Flesh Mountain, ascending hand over fist. When he's near the lowest step, he reaches for it with one hand but misses. The rope swings, rocking him back and forth.

"Goddamnit!" Chuck yells.

"Pops, do you need a hand?"

"No son, I'll be fine, just give me a moment to catch my breath."

Chuck waits for the rope to stop moving then lunges for the step again, this time with both hands. His fingers graze the iron, then slip. He drops backward into the mound below.

"My ankle! I think it's broken!" Chuck yells as he's trying to get up.

"Don't move," Carter shouts down to him. "I'm coming for you right now!"

Carter spits in his palm to add traction for descending the rope, but he's too slow. In a flash, Simon jumps through the utility hole like a damn Ninja Turtle.

"What are you doing?" Carter asks as the little guy scales down the rope. Ignoring him, Simon helps Chuck to his feet, offering his body as a crutch.

"Pops, you okay?"

"Fine son, I have my little friend helping me here," Chuck says, trying to sound cheerful. "But it looks like we've gotta part ways, I'll just slow you down now. I'll get back to the Jeep, just call me when you're ready for me. Now hurry, get my niece!"

Quinn darts up a short flight of stairs and calls to us from the landing, where there's a door, "Follow me." Once we've caught up to him, Quinn opens the door and pokes his face through. He says, "They're not far."

Who the hell are *they*?

26. Cold-blooded Killer

The boiler room opens to a broad hallway that appears preserved from the last day of school —lockers flung open, sheets of loose homework, torn academic books littered on the hardwood floors. A sagging banner pinned to one wall says in orange paint: LET'S GO FALLS, LET'S GO!

"This way," Quinn says, then dashes down the hall to our right. Carter and I sprint to keep up with the quick-moving kid, passing the school's library, music room, and a display case of plaques. I'm out of breath and my sides ache. I can't believe this podunk town's school is so huge.

As I'm rounding a corner, I skid on a textbook and fall. A sharp pain races up my leg. I bellow, "Hold up!"

Carter and Quinn put on the brakes and make their way toward me.

"Are you alright?" Carter asks.

"I slipped on a stupid book," I say, nursing my leg. "I don't think it's sprained or anything. Just give me a second. Quinn, how much further are we—"

THUMP THUMP THUMP!

Steady footsteps resound from somewhere behind us. We whip our heads around and don't see anyone, but the footsteps seem to be getting closer.

The hairs on the back of my neck spring upright. Quinn says, "Over here," running to hide behind a nearby staircase.

Carter throws my arm over his shoulder and helps me stagger over to Quinn. I steady my breath with long exhales. The pain fades as my adrenaline builds in anticipation of what's coming next. We wait and listen, and the footsteps grow louder.

THUMP THUMP!

Through a gap between the risers of the staircase, we have a partial view of the hallway up to the corner where I recently ate shit. Carter unzips his backpack and takes out his roll of duct tape and box cutter. He looks at me and silently mouths, "Take this," pressing the cutter into my palm. It's cold and heavy in my grip.

THUMP THUMP!

Quinn takes off his shoes and yanks the laces

from the worn sneakers. I tap his shoulder and whisper, "What are you doing?" Quinn presses his index finger to his lips.

THUMP THUMP!

An amorphous shadow casts into the hallway, nothing recognizably human. A heartbeat later, its source appears: a gurney piled with bodies. But who's pushing the meat hauler? Noah emerges into the light, rolling the gurney at a measured pace.

Before I can even think about what to do next, Quinn is already advancing toward Noah. He makes his way around the staircase, and barefoot in socks, he's as quiet as an owl in flight. I blink. Quinn is behind Noah. I blink again, and Quinn's shoelaces are around Noah's throat. Holy shit, the kid's an assassin.

Noah gurgles and tries to free himself from the monkey on his back. Carter rushes toward the action. He slaps a chunk of duct tape over Noah's mouth then bears down on his torso, pinning him to the floor. I squeeze the box cutter in my hand and flick out its angled blade, then hesitate. What am I going to do, stab Noah? I'm not a cold-blooded killer. I pocket the cutter and race over to help restrain Noah's thrashing legs by sitting on his kneecaps. Carter wraps Noah's ankles and wrists together with tape, then we drag him and the corpse-piled gurney underneath the staircase.

We inspect the bodies and among them, I notice a familiar face—the gutter punk from jail, the one whose foot I ran over with the Beast. He's cut up to hell, his ribcage torn in half and stripped of organs just like the poor bastards in the drainpipe.

Carter squats down eye level with Noah, who's slumped with his tailbone against the stairs, then motions me over. He sticks his hand out and says, "Cutter." I draw the tool from my pocket and pass it to him. Carter flicks the razor out from its handle and pricks the sharp tip against Noah's chin. "Now listen you worm," he says in a low, threatening voice. "I'm gonna take this tape off, and you're gonna tell me where Sunshine is, you twisted fuck. If you scream or call for help, you're dead. Got that?"

Noah moans incoherently.

Carter rips the tape off his lips and asks, "Now where is she?"

Noah moans again and shakes his head. Carter slaps him across the cheek and hisses, "I won't ask you again!" Noah doesn't say a damn thing. His pupils are dilated, giant empty holes of nothingness.

Carter raises the cutter, ready to stab. I drop a knee to Noah and tell him, "Look at me." His eyeballs begin to spin in counterclockwise circles. What's wrong with him? He looks like he's high out of his mind. I ask, "Where's Jim? Where's Sheriff Evans?"

Noah mumbles a bunch of vowels then falls forward, face smacking against the floor.

Carter shakes his head and says, "We don't have time for this bullshit."

Quinn kneels by us and takes the cutter from Carter's fist. In one quick motion, he shreds the razor blade across the back of Noah's neck. Noah jerks upright, screaming with blood gushing out of him as if he were a busted sewer pipe. Carter slaps the duct tape back over his mouth, muffling his cries.

Quinn drops the blade and squeezes the fresh incision as if popping a zit. He jams his fingers into Noah's flesh and fishes around. Seconds later, he triumphantly holds up a small bloody object the size of a postage stamp.

I look closer. It's a *microchip*.

Quinn uses the butt end of the box cutter to smash the silicon chip to smithereens, then returns the tool to Carter. He stands and tells us, "He's better now."

"What the fuck was that?" Carter mumbles.

Noah's eyes flutter open, their color returning to blue as his pupils contract to a normal size. He swallows, then in a faint, raspy voice, he says, "Thank you." Then his body folds to the floor like an accordion.

"Noah!" I cry. There's no response. I check his pulse. He's breathing.

BEEP! BEEP!

Suddenly a high-pitched alarm begins to shriek through the halls, accompanied by white strobe lights flashing from all directions.

Quinn yells, "Run!"

27. Fresh trail of blood

The deafening alarm masks the pounding of our footsteps as Carter and I once more strive to match pace with Quinn. I huff and puff, sounding like a fat kid after running a mile. I have no clue where Quinn is leading us, and not enough breath to ask. Unexpectedly, he comes to an abrupt halt, his heels firmly planting on the ground. Carter and I catch up to him and find that he's standing before a set of sturdy double doors with a single word spray painted across them in red: ESSENTIALS.

A loud chorus of wails from beyond the doors rises like a demented choir warming up for rehearsal, audible even over the continuing alarm. I back away in horror.

Carter asks, panting for breath, "She's ... in ... there?"

Quinn shrugs. "Lots of people in there."

Quinn swings the doors open, and my mouth drops to the floor. Inside, a school gymnasium has been transformed into what resembles a nightmarish field hospital. To my left, rows of people are bound to gurneys, undergoing blood extraction. To my right, hundreds of deputies stand together in tan uniforms, all of their heads freshly shaven. It becomes clear that they're the source of the infernal chorus. Moaning bizarrely and swaying strangely like sunflowers in a field, they seem oblivious to our entrance.

We pause for a few heartbeats, but it soon becomes clear that the deputies are no threat to us. They appear to be in some kind of hypnotic state. Stealthily, Carter and I dash for the rows of gurneys and begin to search for Sunshine.

The tied-down people are unconscious with tubes in their arms filling blood bags. Some are covered by bleached white sheets while others are exposed, showing massive black stitches across their stomachs and chests, slathered with a thick layer of clear gel. A strong earthy scent lingers in the air. I move through the rows of gurneys, scanning the faces. Most are strangers, some are not. One is Tanya. Damn, she used to hand deliver my mail at work. Another is a regular from my clinic, Phil. So far, no Sunshine.

At the end of the rows, something catches my

eye—a familiar splash of magenta light radiates from behind a wall of curtains. I'm drawn toward the glow. I pull the curtain back to see, to my astonishment, the therapy lights from my clinic. By reflex I shove my face close to one, shut my eyes, and let the rays soak into my skin.

Oh man, it's been too long and it feels so fucking good. Thick layers of stress and pain melt off me. It's like I'm dancing in a grassy field, barefoot, laughing underneath a cloudless sky. I could stand here and soak up these soothing rays forever. They feel like sun—

Sunshine! My eyes burst open. What am I doing?

I gather myself. My lights are on C-stands, pointing down at a woman lying on a medical bed with a ventilator over her face. Her exposed skin is covered in clear goo. Three tubes are attached to her body, with a line in each arm and a third behind her left ear. The tubes flow into a sizable blood bag on a hook. On the bag is Sharpied: PERFECT O-.

My breath catches in my throat when I see a familiar wedding band on the woman's hand, studded with sapphires. I rush closer and look through the clear plastic shield of the ventilator. Fuck me, I'd know that face anywhere.

"Mom! It's me, Max!" I yell, but she's unresponsive. I grab her wrist to check her pulse, and she has a slow yet steady heartbeat. She's alive. I kiss my mother's hand, whisper "I'll come back for you," and take off to continue my search.

I track down Carter. He's shoving his way through the deputies like a Walmart shopper on Black Friday while hollering Sunshine's name. I notice the deputies have stitches on the back of their clean-shaven necks, just like Noah and Junior. Among them I see Deputy Asshole, now drooling and swaying like the others. There are even more faces I recognize from town, such as a waiter from the Horseshoe, the manager of the Mount Baker Theater, and Larry. They for sure weren't deputies a few days ago.

"Sunshine!" Carter and I scream, but the deputies' wails drown out our weaker voices. Then, as if someone flipped a switch, both the alarm and the moanings stop. The gym falls silent, and the deputies all twist around toward us in unison. Carter and I look at each other like deer in headlights. Then the deputies charge.

Time slows as we swing our fists, trying to fight them off. It's no use; our attackers aren't fast, but they're relentless and there's too many of them. They seize us by our limbs and force us to the floor.

Then, as fast as the mob attacked, they freeze as if playing a recess game of Red Light Green Light. Their hands unlatch from my clothing, and they stiffen back into their weird sunflowers-swaying-in-the-breeze act.

Then, the sound of a pair of hands clapping reverberates through the gymnasium. It's that obnoxious, sarcastic kind of slow clap. I scramble to my feet, brush myself off, and look for the source of the sound. It's fucking Sheriff Evans, and he's in the corner of the gym near the curtains that divide my mother's bed from the others. He grins and holds up a silver box about the size of a deck of cards. He presses a button on the box—CLICK!—and the deputies shuffle aside into two neat lines to either side of us.

Evans says, "Max. You must have nine lives." He tilts back his cowboy hat from his forehead.

"Where is she?" I yell.

"Who? Your mother? She's here, dumbass." Evans points toward the curtains next to him. "Should I check in on her, you think?"

"Don't fucking touch her, you sack of shit!" I scream, rushing toward him. Evans holds up his silver box and says, "I wouldn't come any closer if I were you, Max. Not if you want your mother to make it through the night."

I stop in my tracks. Behind me, Carter says, "Where's Sunshine, you sick fuck? Tell me or I'll fucking kill you with my bare hands!"

Evans chuckles. "Wow. Big words from a little bald boy. Max, tell your boyfriend what I told you

... If you don't keep quiet, I'll have my size sixteen boot up both your asses so quick your heads will spin."

CLICK!

The deputies are now looking at us, heads cocked and mouths drooling as if they're zombies and it's lunchtime at Oak Falls High.

Evans continues, "Man, do I love this technology. You know fellas, this beautiful little transmitter is the same shit they use down in their coffee bean farms. Keeps 'em pickin' all day without complaining. Ha! You're looking at my army here. Hundreds of what used to be pathetic nonessential ass-clowns are now mine, and I'm working them around the clock, making sure you stupid fuckos stay indoors. Ha! I tell them when to move, when to eat, when to shit, when to sleep!"

CLICK!

The deputies twinge and jerk, then one of them lurches at me and pins me to the ground, rendering me helpless. Carter pulls out his box cutter and swipes it across the back of my assailant's neck, then quickly rips out another bloody microchip. The deputy releases me and crumples to the floor. One of the other mind-controlled minions knocks the blade from Carter's grip and it clatters away, spinning end over end.

BANG!

I turn to see Evans holding his smoking six-shooter above his head. "Next one goes between your mother's ears, Max," Evans says. "What you just experienced is a fraction of this new technology's potential strength. You see, control is power and I'm a god under this new world order. I'll be damned if you two dingleberries are gonna stop me!"

Quinn comes out of nowhere, darting silently toward Evans with Carter's box cutter held in his grip like a spear. He leaps into the air, soaring, but Evans sidesteps with unexpected grace. Quinn misses his target but is able to knock the transmitter out of his hand.

BANG!

Quinn drops like a rock, holding his stomach, bleeding. Evans stands above him, pointing his pistol at the kid's head. He says, "Quinn, you dumbass. Shouldn't you be working in the pit with your dipshit brothers? Sorry, I mean, brother, ha!"

"Fuck ... you," Quinn gasps, then starts to make a noise like he's crying. What sounds like sobs at first gets louder, and it becomes clear that he's laughing like a crazed hyena.

"Oh, you think this is funny?" Evans says, sounding pissed. "Well, this shit ain't the Sunday cartoons, you backstabbing little ginger shit!"

BANG!

Evans sends a slug into Quinn's brain. The

kid's laughter stops and I freeze in place, shocked by Quinn's bloody end.

The fat bastard Evans picks up his silver device and presses a button. CLICK!

I brace myself for attacks from all sides. Instead, the deputies ignore me and Carter and begin to shove each other, lightly at first, then soon the gym becomes a giant mosh pit as they slam into one another. Evans fiddles with his transmitter as if trying to fix it, scowling and cursing.

Carter sprints toward Evans, dodging and hurdling over deputies and gurneys, and surprises him by jumping on his back. Evans bucks wildly like a raging bull trying to throw off a cowboy at a rodeo. He empties his clip—BANG! BANG! BANG!—he's trying to shoot Carter but misses and only takes out a couple of his own deputies, including Deputy Asshole.

I snap out of my shock and run toward them. Evans has Carter pinned on his back with his size sixteen boot on his chest. Before I can reach them, Evans raises his leg and smashes his boot into my friend's rib cage. Carter shrieks in agony. A soggy rag falls to the floor from his hand. I dive for the rag just as a flailing deputy collides into Evans, knocking him down.

Spinning and ducking away from more of the deputies, I straddle Evans's back. Reaching around, I smother his face with the chemical-soaked cloth. He kicks and squirms and tries to get away, but I don't let go. I use all my strength to keep the rag over his mouth and nostrils, trying to suffocate him.

Evans changes his tactic, and instead of trying to fight me off he scrabbles desperately for his silver box, but it's lying out of his reach. I can feel his muscles weaken. His hands go limp and his head slumps, his neck no longer able to support the weight. His squirms become fewer and lighter, then none. I yank his handcuffs from his utility belt and snap the cold metal rings over his wrists. I tell him, "Looks like you're in the trunk."

I dismount from his back and snatch up the transmitter. I study the interface, a monochromatic screen with an array of buttons. I press one labeled STANDBY.

CLICK!

The deputies stop clashing and stiffen in place once again. I slip the transmitter into my coveralls' back pocket and make my way toward Carter. I pass Quinn's body, lying in a puddle of his blood. I kneel down and release the box cutter from his death grip. I hesitate then, looking back toward the unconscious sheriff.

"I'm sorry Quinn, but I'm not a killer," I tell him regretfully. "I'll make sure Evans gets what he deserves."

I hear moaning. I look up and see Carter

trying to get to his feet. "My ribs," he whimpers. "That fucker—"

"Don't move or you'll make it worse," I say. He nods with his teeth clenched, eyes shut. I hurry to his side. "Where's your phone?" I ask.

Carter's trembling hand points at his backpack. I pick it up and pluck out his cell phone. "Call your Pops and let him know we're inside the gymnasium. Don't forget my mom, she's behind those curtains." I shove the phone into his hand. "And record video of this fucked-up place. Can you do that?"

Carter has to suck up some snot through his nasal cavity before he can respond. He says, "I got you."

"Carter, you gotta stay strong, okay? Stay strong while I go find your cuz."

He nods, his eyes squinting from excruciating pain.

"Good. And keep this for protection while I'm gone," I say, handing him his box cutter. "These deputy-fucks might go berserk again."

"Max," Carter says, "I fucking hate the Falls."

"You and me both, brother," I tell him.

I leave Carter and walk toward my mother's bed to check on her. I pull back the curtains and am greeted by the sight of magenta lights illuminating nothing at all. She's gone.

I scour the immediate area, thinking that

maybe her bed got bumped around during the recent fray. I soon realize that someone's taken her. On the floor where her bed used to be, I detect a fresh trail of blood leading to an emergency exit door. I follow the drops.

28. The pink crap

I keep my head down and eyes peeled wide open as I pursue the trail of drops like a bloodhound. It leads me through another hallway, past lockers and plaques, and shit, I realize I've been moving in a circle. I've lost the scent and now I haven't got a clue where to go next.

I think to myself that maybe I should consider a different plan. Maybe I should just go back to the gym and check in with Carter, or I could check the parking lot, and shit, I've gotta find Sunshine too, hell maybe she's—

I hear screaming.

The cries lead me back to Noah where we left him in the stairwell. He's sitting curled up into a ball, not looking so hot. He's sticky with sweat, skin blanched, teetering between a state of consciousness and death.

I crouch down and ask, "Noah, can you hear me?"

He runs his shaky fingers through his greasy blond hair and mumbles, "Who are you? Where ... am ... I? How did I get here?"

"I'm Max, and you're at Oak Falls High School. Don't worry. You're gonna be okay now."

"I ... I ... am?" he stutters, then goes limp.

"Noah." I shake him. "Wake up."

He moans and coughs up spit and snot.

"Noah, listen to me. Tell me—where's Jim?"

He mutters incoherently then slumps to one side. I press my finger against his throat. He's breathing.

There's blood spattered on the floor by Noah, and I assume at first that it's from the cut in his neck. But then I realize that they're fresh, brighter red than the blood crusted on his neck. I pick up the trail once more.

It continues up the staircase to a short hallway with a familiar earthy scent. I follow the drops to a door labeled SCIENCE LAB 1. I push the door open to a flood of blue lights and a blast of heat. "Sunshine!" I call out, taking a step inside.

The room reeks of compost and is crammed with enormous aloe vera plants sprouting from horse troughs. Reflective silver sheets line the lab's walls, duct taped along the seams, and industrial fans along the perimeter blow the hot air around.

Off to one side is a table that holds Bunsen burners heating jars of chopped leaves in liquid, and piled below are boxes labeled MEDICINE.

"Sunshine!" No response.

The plants in this lab are stunningly vibrant, even larger than the ones I saw in Sunshine's barn. Despite my urgency, I pause to marvel at their prehistoric scale. My eyes move down one spiky leaf to its base and spot something protruding from the soil. Gum?

I pluck up the sticky object, wipe off the excess dirt, then hold it up in the light. It's half of a human ear. I drop it, horrified.

THUD!

It sounds like a car door slamming outside. I cross the lab and press my face against a window. Looking down at the fresh-fallen snow in the parking lot below, I spot bloody footprints leading from the building to Jim, who's standing at the rear doors of my Beast. Flurries drift around him as if he's inside a shaken snow globe. Furious, I beat the glass with my elbow. His head snaps back and our eyes meet, his mouth crooks into a smirk, then that fucker flips me the bird with both hands. He hops into the driver's seat, revs the engine, and peels out in my Beast!

My temperature skyrockets and I imagine myself breaking the window glass, jumping over the ledge, and hunting that bastard down. But the fantasy dissipates at a creaking sound from behind me. I turn. Across the room is Sunshine, covered in a bloody apron and carrying a gallon-size ziplock bag filled with pink mush.

"Sunshine, we've been looking all over for you!" I cry out, overjoyed. "Come on, let's get you out of here." She ignores me and dumps the pink crap at the base of an aloe plant. She then shuffles away through a door marked SCIENCE LAB 2.

Weaving through the room between troughs, I barge into the second lab, but I don't see her anywhere. I look around, frantically calling out her name.

This lab is filled with refrigerators lining its walls as though it were a Home Depot kitchen showroom. Some of the appliances have stickers of local business logos—the Horseshoe and Larry's Donut Shop. I pause to open one of the fridges—fuck me, it's Jeffrey Dahmer's wet dream. It's stuffed to the brim with jarred human organs and blood.

I unlatch one more, then another, and they're all the same until I reach one large split-door refrigerator labeled with the word HOLTZ. When I open this one, I can't believe what I see. Where you would expect to be shelves and bins, the inside has been gutted and opens to a tunnel lit with a string of Christmas lights.

I walk into the tunnel and follow the red,

green, and gold bulbs, hollering Sunshine's name, but all I hear are my own echoes. I'm alone and it feels like I'm hallucinating, or dreaming. Some dream, more like a fucking nightmare.

The tunnel spits me out into a brick-walled hallway, lit by the same holiday lights. To my right is a chained door, and to my left are piles of stiffs looking like mummies wrapped in cellophane. Some are on gurneys, while others are scattered on the floor. What the fu—

CRRSSSHK!

A mechanical grinding sound emanates from down the hall, past the stiffs.

CRRRSSSSHHHKK!

I cover my ears with my hands and move toward the deafening sound, stepping over the shrink-wrapped corpses. My boot tears a piece of cellophane, and clear goo oozes from the rip.

CRSSRSSSSSHHHNNNK!

I reach a sheet of perforated plastic, push through, and I'm in a brick room with more refrigerators tagged with the word HOLTZ. Next to them are several pink-stained buckets, and there's Sunshine to my far right. She's on a stubby stepladder beside an industrial-size meat grinder, and—*holy shitballs*—she's forcing a human leg into its jumbo hopper. Pink mush pours from the grinder's spout into a five-gallon bucket labeled FERTILIZER.

"Sunshine!" I shout, but she doesn't respond. I notice a thick electrical cord snaking from the meat grinder. I run toward it and give it a firm tug, but it doesn't budge. I trace the cord to where it disappears behind a fridge and shove the appliance over. It lands on its side and its doors fling open, spilling out a cascade of organs. I rip the cord from the exposed wall outlet. The grinder rumbles to a stop.

I look back at Sunshine and see that she's off the ladder and writing on a clipboard. I'm struck by a morbid urge to look inside the meat grinder. I step up the ladder and lean over the hopper. At the bottom, I see a mangled finger with a ring still attached, glinting with sapphires—it's my mother's fucking wedding ring.

"Sunshine! What the fuck did you do?"

She ignores me and continues to scribble on her clipboard. It's at this moment I finally realize—she's chipped. I hurtle down the steps and reach toward her neck, looking for the telltale stitches. Sunshine drops the clipboard and takes a swing at me with the pen clenched like a dagger in her fist. I take a step back, and the pen slices through empty air. She strikes again, and this time she manages to rip my coveralls.

"Stop it!" I beg her, but she's not listening and continues to come at me. I backpedal, doing my best to evade her sweeping hooks. My ass bumps against a brick wall, and the impact reminds me of what's in my butt pocket. I pull out the silver transmitter. Bingo! I point it at her, push the button marked STANDBY, and wait.

Nothing happens and she keeps coming at me. She catches me off my guard and stabs me in the side with the ballpoint. AAAAHHHH! Fuck, that hurts. I look down, and there's a fucking J & J on the shaft of the pen.

I drop the silver box and push her off me. Sunshine slips on the guts that spilled from the fridge and tumbles down. I rip the pen from my side, kneel on Sunshine's back, and flip her hair over to one side, exposing the back of her neck. I was right—fresh stitches. I tear the tip of the pen through the stitches, brutally splitting them apart. She kicks and yowls like a stray cat but I'm beyond caring, and I dig my fingers deep until I feel the microchip buried in her flesh. I claw it out and snap it in half. Sunshine goes limp.

I get off her. She lies there for a moment, still on her stomach as her breath becomes more steady. Her fingers rise to her neck and run against her fresh wound, then she sits up, trembling. Her eyes meet mine and her lips quiver open.

"Max?"

29. Epilogue: Zonk off to La-La Land

Three days have passed, and I'm in a recovery room at the St. Joseph Medical Hospital in Bellingham with Sunshine, Carter, Chuck, and that little ginger Simon—we've nicknamed him Crutch.

Chuck is recovering from a liver transplant and ankle surgery. The doctors had plenty of livers to choose from at the school. They say he should be able to go home in a few more days, but he'll need around-the-clock care for weeks.

Right now, Carter is sleeping on a bed beside his Pops. He's got a cast around his cracked ribs that he has to wear for a while, but he'll live.

Crutch is a nice addition to our crew, and one tough kid too. He single-handedly helped Chuck to his Jeep, then drove—for his first time—to the school and helped us to the hospital.

The Nonessentials

Sunshine's neck is healing and she could have left the hospital yesterday, but she won't leave our sides. She feels horrible for what she's done, and I've been telling her it's not her fault that she ground my mother into mush. She was chipped, after all.

Mother. *Fuck.* To tell you the truth, I've been a wreck. It wasn't until early this morning that I've gotten a solid grip on my sanity, and although her death has torn a hole in my heart, I've been trying to make peace with the fact that she is in a—wait! Fuck that noise. Those bastards are going to pay.

Let's back up a few days. So, after leaving the school, I called the Feds with Carter's phone—pressing star-sixty-seven first, of course. I told them the whole story, about the bodies, the school, the guts, all of it. They didn't believe me. At least, not until I sent them a clip from Carter's phone. They came, they saw, and oh boy did they conquer. They had a field day with the local law enforcement's mess.

Right now, the Feds have Evans and Noah in their custody, among others. Noah will probably get off the hook but Evans, that tub of lard, he's going to live out his days in a cement cell.

Then there's Jim and Junior. Those turds are on the run and last I heard, heading south in my beloved Beast. It boils me to think that those bastards are free and driving her around. *F!U!C!K!*

I can't think about it too much right now. The doctors say that my blood pressure is through the roof. *Breathe.*

There's one more thing—the SD card I swallowed at Chuck's place. What was on it has made international news. Its files contained evidence about how the largest coffee company in the world struck a deal with Anderson Paper Mill. Turns out that months ago, Governor Holtz's husband Mr. Holtz, a.k.a. Seattle coffee tycoon Holtz, purchased toilet paper from the defunct mill at pennies on the dollar purely to turn them into cheap coffee filters for all seven hundred of his Washington State cafes. Sunshine was right. The mill was full of deadly levels of mercury, and when the contaminated filters flooded the java shops, people started dying of organ failure from fucking mercury poisoning, not some made-up disease called HIT.

And I'm not finished ... Mr. Holtz and his entire family clan became sick from the tainted coffee, so like the many thousands of others he poisoned, their essential organs started failing—and fast. It was challenging, which Dr. Howson explains in an email found on the SD card, to find suitable donors for immediate transplants. And that's when Governor Holtz stepped in. She hired Evans to capture potential donors under the premise of Phase Zero, and Jim to harvest and stockpile O- essentials. They had a hard time keeping the organs fresh and the donors alive until they got a hold of Sunshine's aloe vera. She was right again—it does repair damaged cells.

Fucking hell, what an utter shitstorm it's been. It's getting late and I need some shut-eye, but before I zonk off to la-la land, there's one final tidbit I'd like to share that makes me personally proud. The Feds locked up my stolen therapy lights for evidence and said that it would be a long time before I'd see them again, but get this: I told them great, I don't care, keep them for as long as you like because I don't need them anymore.

Sunshine is the only medicine I need.

Acknowledgments

I'm incredibly grateful for the support I've received on my writing journey. Elliot, Lisa, Gail, Rick, Henry, and the entire WRT crew, your feedback on my early chapters was invaluable. Sharon Stogner and Minae Lee, your editing skills were pivotal. Thanks to everyone for putting up with my antics.

About the Author

Zachary worked in the film industry until the pandemic, during which he moved corpses for a mortuary. He lives in Arizona, where he's creating extraordinary nonsense from inside air-controlled spaces. *The Nonessentials* is his debut novel.

Printed in the USA
CPSIA information can be obtained
at www.ICGtesting.com
LVHW091040150224
771651LV00005B/162